"I want to kiss you

Maybe it was the magical glen, where it was said the fairy folk came in closest contact, that triggered her response. As he silently thanked the magical beings, Nolan reacted to her tremulous words. As their mouths touched, Nolan felt a bolt of lightning erupt through him. Heat followed the flash through his body.

A moan rose from Kendra as he took her like a warrior would take his woman. His mouth was strong, cherishing and hungry. Drowning in his strength, his mouth wreaking havoc within her heated body, Kendra wondered if they had a second chance with one another.

She trusted Nolan again with her life—as she had before. And yet, she also wondered if she was headed for an even bigger fall....

LINDSAY McKENNA

is part Eastern Cherokee and has walked the path of her ancestors, through her father's training. Her "other" name is Ai Gvhdi Waya—Walks With Wolves. When she was nine, Lindsay's father began to teach her the "medicine" ways, or skills brought down through their family lineage. For nine years Lindsay remained in training. There was never a name given to what was handed down through her Wolf Clan family lines, but nowadays it is generally called shamanism. Having grown up in a Native American environment, Lindsay is close to Mother Earth and all her relations. She has taught interested people around the globe about how to reconnect spiritually with the earth. She is now infusing her books with her many years of experiences and metaphysical knowledge in hope that readers will discover a newfound awe for the magic that is around us in our everyday reality. She considers herself a metaphysician, and her intent is to bring compassion and "heart" through her storytelling, for she believes the greatest healer of them all is love.

LINDSAY McKENNA

THE QUEST

Silhouette Books

nocturne™

 SILHOUETTE BOOKS

ISBN-13: 978-0-373-61780-7
ISBN-10:   0-373-61780-1

THE QUEST

Dear Reader,

The Quest is book three from the *WARRIORS FOR THE LIGHT* series. Join me as Kendra Johnson and Nolan Galloway, archaeologists with a strong personal history, team up to find the third emerald sphere. What is it like to work closely with someone you once loved? That is the dilemma Kendra is faced with regarding Nolan. Worse, arch villain Victor Carancho Guerra and his dark empire reveal more of his own search for the emerald sphere. He is the most dangerous person in spirit and will kill without forethought to get the sphere first.

Their archaeological hunger to find something as rare and important as the emerald sphere drives Nolan and Kendra. They work for the Vesica Piscis Foundation in Ecuador (run by Reno Manchahi and Calen Hernandez of *Unforgiven*, the first book of the series). Kendra and Nolan must grit their teeth for a higher calling and try to make an archaeological find that will stun the world—while ignoring the smoldering embers of their love, which refuses to die.

Come along with me as *The Quest* unfolds. I love to hear from my readers, and you can contact me at http://www.lindsaymckenna.com. And, join my list at http://lists.topica.com/lists/lm/. I enjoy interacting with my readers, so let me hear from you.

Warmly,

Lindsay McKenna

To Verde Valley Medical Center, Cottonwood, Arizona: Dr. Barbara Braun of the ER, the social workers and the Cottonwood floor nurses station. Thank you for your compassion in taking care of my mother, Ruth. I'm indebted to you for your humanity toward her during one of her darkest hours. And to RTA Hospice of Sedona, Arizona, who have been an incredible emotional support team to us and our family, as well as to our mother. To OJ, Susan B., Holly, Jericho, Rosemarie, Terry and so many more that I have failed to name but are equally important to us, thank you. Your compassion, swiftness of reaction, and being there for us have been such a blessing. You are a magnificent organization and I hope more people consider hospice for their loved ones who must, one day, pass on.

ACKNOWLEDGMENTS

I want to thank the Web site http://www.cropcircleconnector.com for its incredible and inspiring photographs of the amazing crop circles in southwestern England. And thank you to the Wiltshire Crop Circle Study Group at http://www.wccsg.com for their excellent newsletter, *The Sprial*. Special thanks goes to an article by Horace Drew on the "Wormhole Energy Machines" (November 2006 Issue 123) and editor Francine Blake.

And, to my crop circle adventuring companion, Michele Burdet of Chesieres, Switzerland, who is renowned for her dowsing abilities: We had a lot of fascinating discoveries and mind-boggling experiences as we walked the sacred crop circles together in 2004. I thank her for her information, intuitive ability and provocative theories about these magical symbols.

Prologue

"Nolan, are you sure you can get us to that archaeological site?"

Nolan Galloway sat at the rear of a small inflatable yellow raft designed to float down the restless Colorado River. They were deep in the mile-high Grand Canyon with red, white, purple and orange layers of rock rising on either side of them. As beautiful as the canyon was, his focus was fixed on what he considered the eighth wonder of the world: Kendra Johnson. And he was engaged to her! His heart swelled with such a fierce love for her that he was momentarily at a loss for words. That didn't happen often.

"Sure, I'm sure, earth woman," Nolan teased her with a confident grin. He had two endearments for his fiancée and this was one of them. The other was decidedly Irish—"darlin'." Kendra was half-Navajo, and her roots were with her mother's people in the Southwest, even though her renowned archaeologist father had come from Ireland.

"I've run this canyon at least forty times," Nolan told her. "It's a piece of cake." He stared into her dark green eyes, which reminded him of the sun slanting through a forest on a bright, cloudless afternoon. Doubt registered in her expression. This was the first time Kendra had rafted with him to the dig located about four miles inside the canyon.

Mouth quirking with uncertainty, Kendra glanced over at the third passenger, her younger sister, Debby. Right now the Colorado looked glassy and smooth, the water murky because of all the silt carried along with it. Sunlight danced off the surface, providing a magical effect.

Debby seemed worried, her smooth brow furrowed. She probably didn't want to voice her concerns.

"I hear a roar ahead, Nolan. Is that rapids?" Kendra pressed.

"Sure is. Relax. It's midsummer and the rapids aren't dangerous like they are in spring, when snow-melt makes them higher. The river is at its lowest point now." Nolan watched the warm July wind caress Kendra's shoulder-length red hair, which gleamed with gold and purple highlights. She wore a sensible straw hat with a wide brim, but it didn't hide those Irish freckles that spilled across her nose and high cheekbones.

His body responded hotly when their eyes met. He wished he could climb across the raft, which was loaded with a week's worth of camping gear, food and archaeological equipment, and take her in his arms. If he could hug her, reassure her, she'd be able to relax and enjoy the canyon's inspiring beauty, he knew.

It wasn't like Kendra to be this worried, but Nolan figured she was being protective of Debby, her only sibling. Debby was going to Harvard, planning to follow the family tradition and become an archaeologist. This was her first dig experience. It was something Kendra wanted to do for Debby: show her life as a working archaeologist, out in nature and braving the elements. For Kendra, the class time and studying was worth it. Archaeology was a magical and exciting adventure.

Nolan gave Kendra a wink, and her cheeks colored prettily. She often blushed when he looked at her, telling her with a bold glance that he loved her. Kendra was well on her way to tenure at Harvard, and carried herself with pride and reserve, as she thought a professor should. She blamed his less-serious, often teasing demeanor on him graduating from Princeton, not from Harvard, the undisputed king of academia.

But then, Nolan reminded himself, that was one of the many reasons Kendra loved him. He was animated and playful, a real extrovert. They balanced one another nicely, Nolan felt.

At age twenty-seven, he held the world in his hands, because he had Kendra's love. He had fallen hopelessly in love soon after meeting her, and they had big plans for their future. In four months, they would marry.

"Those rapids are about half a mile long. They'll be tame," he assured both sisters. Nolan saw Debby frown and the thick rope fastened around the top of the raft as a safety line. Kendra had warned him that Debby was not a good swimmer. He'd persuaded the love of his life that her sister was going to be safe on this trip. Oh, they might get a little spray from running the rapids, but that was all. Pretty tame stuff as far as Nolan was concerned.

He gave Debby a thumbs-up, keeping his other hand on the wooden rudder that guided the inflatable raft down the river. Debby smiled weakly in return.

They all wore life vests, a must for rafting the mighty and quixotic Colorado. Nolan figured that, even in a worst-case scenario, they'd bob like corks through the rapids. He knew from many trips down this river that the current was deep and powerful. Only strong swimmers who knew not to fight the current should venture in. But between the rapids were wide sandbars and quieter water. All a person had to do was float through the turbulent waves and paddle toward shore. It might take anywhere from a quarter to a full mile to reach the shallows, but eventually one would. That was the only way to negotiate the mighty river, which cut like a knife through the glorious multicolored layers of exposed rock. Nolan had schooled both women in the procedure—just in case.

Kendra gazed about, feeling comforted by Nolan's jovial words and the confidence he exuded about running the rapids. The beauty around her was breathtaking. Gray sandbars, perhaps fifty feet away on either side, glistened with gold specks. Above them the yellowish Muav limestone and brownish-gray Tapeats sandstone rose majestically.

She was excited to be on a dig with Nolan. Harvard and Princeton were jointly underwriting the project, which dealt with early Native American settlers in the canyon. Kendra glowed inwardly when she caught Nolan's penetrating gaze. He made love with her like a musician playing an instrument. The symphonies they made together were exquisite, reminding her of the passionate thunderstorms when Father Sky loved Mother Earth.

The roar of the rapids grew louder as Nolan guided the small raft toward the next curve of the canyon. Kendra glanced at her sister, who had a scowl on her face, her lips set in obvious tension. Debby was obviously scared and she couldn't blame her. Kendra had never rafted down the Colorado, either, but she was a strong swimmer, so being on water didn't bother her. Still, Nolan's instructions at Lees Ferry, where they'd launched the raft had been frightening even to her. He'd explained about the strong current, the powerful undertows that could suck a swimmer down.

Kendra dragged in a deep breath as the thunder of the rapids grew steadily louder. The white water must begin right around the next corner, a point of jutting white rock. The deep rumbling was a warning to all rafters to beware. Grabbing the thick rope on the edge of the raft, she braced herself for the coming rapids. Nolan had assured them the set would be tame compared to how it was in spring runoff.

Kendra gasped in surprise as they rounded the corner. The rapids stretched from one side of the river to the other, and the waves were huge! Green water glinted in the sun, breaking into spray as it washed up and over boulders. The churning white water went on for as far as she could see.

"Hold on!" Nolan shouted, as he gripped the rudder more surely. "We're going in!" He loved this group of rapids. The water level was a little higher than he'd expected. Heavy thunderstorms in the mountains would often dump inches of water that would hours later wash unexpectedly into the Colorado. The green river had a reddish tint to it from the silt. Clearly, there had been monsoon activity, for the river was stirred up. The roar was so loud that even as he shouted to the women, he doubted they heard him. Debby was crouched down, hanging on to the rope for dear life.

The raft hit the first of the rapids. Spray slammed into the nose and their vessel was lifted upward. Nolan grinned in exhilaration. Though Debby screamed, and Kendra hunkered down, he didn't fear for them. He had run these rapids many times and could skillfully steer the craft through them using the rudder.

The raft bobbed violently up and down, swaying from side to side. Nolan kept his feet braced on the bottom, his grip strong and sure. Things were going well as they made the next turn, and he grinned again. He loved the fierce power of the Colorado, the cold, numbing spray and the wild, tumbling ride on the ever-changing current.

But then something terrible happened. Ahead, above the churning waves, Nolan spotted, too late, a new boulder. One that had tumbled into the river from a thousand feet above them, changing the course of the current. The red rock, the size of two semi-trucks, loomed out of the water, its jagged edges racing toward them.

With a gasp, Nolan jerked the rudder to the left to try and evade the obstacle. Too late! He heard Debby scream again. Kendra threw her arm across her face as the nose of the craft slammed into the rock.

In seconds, the raft was torn apart. Nolan shouted to the women, but his cry was drowned out by the roar around them. Icy water rushed over the side of the listing inflatable, and seconds later, they were all tossed into the wild, bone-chilling water.

Kendra shrieked and launched herself out of the raft. The water hit her like a wall. Stunned, she felt herself being grabbed by the current near the huge, jagged rock. Somehow, she managed to twist herself around to see Debby being dragged beneath the surface.

There was a whirlpool beside the massive boulder! Kendra struggled to grab on to the rock. The force of the water held her captive against it, the cold shocking her. Nolan had washed downstream with the raft and shouldn't help her.

She saw her sister's frantic wave, and screamed her name. This couldn't be happening! Fighting desperately, Kendra managed to crawl toward the whirlpool. There was no sign of Debby.

No! Kendra pushed forward and felt the sudden grip of the whirling, counterclockwise current. She had on hiking boots, and it seemed as if watery hands were grabbing them and dragging her under. She drew a deep breath, not fighting the current. Instead she allowed it to pull her deeper. She had to find Debby!

Opening her eyes underwater was a huge mistake. Instantly, the gritty silt burned like sandpaper. Shutting her eyelids, she flinched in pain as she gripped the rock with one hand and reached out in desperation with the other. She had to find Debby! Kendra's lungs began to burn. She knew she had to surface, but could she? With no rescue coming, she kicked violently, trying to escape the pull of the current.

Finally, she burst above the surface with a raw and guttural gasp. Again she clung to the rock, the water pounding her unrelentingly and trapping her against it. The sharp shards jabbed and punched at her, bruising her repeatedly.

"Debby!" Kendra shrieked.

The river drowned out her cry.

Fighting the turbulence, Kendra twisted once more. She saw Nolan struggling to swim toward her. He had been swept downstream from where she was trapped. She saw terror on his ashen face. There was a deep cut on his brow and blood was running from his nose.

Everything slowed down and became a blur. Kendra saw no sign of her sister. Her eyes were smarting and tears flowed freely down her face. Her heart was pounding as she gasped for breath. Where was Debby? The thought of losing her baby sister, whom she loved more than life, was unbearable. It couldn't happen!

Kendra didn't care if she lost her own life trying to save her sister. Taking a huge gulp of air into her lungs, she allowed the swirling water to suck her back down. She knew whirlpools were deadly, but she also knew how to get out of them. Debby did not. Kendra kept a death grip on the wall of rock so that she could resurface.

Eyes tightly shut, she felt the silt prickle her face and neck. As hopeless as it seemed, she groped repeatedly through the frigid water, trying to feel her sister. Kendra had no idea how deep the whirlpool was, but she had to go farther down. Debby couldn't die! Not like this! The two of them had already lost their parents in an auto crash on the reservation two years ago. That was when Kendra had taken Debby under her wing. Feeling responsible as never before, she gripped the rock and inched downward.

But just as Kendra reached out once more, a floating log clipped her outstretched arm. Pain shot up through her shoulder and spread into her body. The log was large and smashed into the rock beside her. Kendra couldn't see it, but felt some of the branches pin her in place. Air rushed out of her lungs as they scraped her torso. She was trapped!

Icy terror shot through her. She was caught in the branches, pressed against the rock wall. The whirlpool tugged violently at her feet, and she was running out of air. With panic, Kendra realized she was likely to drown herself. A deep anguish flowed through her as her lungs began to burn like fire. The need to inhale was overwhelming.

Desperate now, Kendra realized the power of the

water was holding the tree against the rock, and it wasn't going to move. She had to escape, or else!

Somehow, with superhuman strength from one last adrenaline rush, she managed to yank herself free of the limbs that enveloped her. The rocks scored her back, and she heard a roaring in her ears. Kendra knew she had brief seconds before she'd inhale a lungful of water and drown.

Lifting her feet, she planted her boots against the rock wall. With one last powerful lunge, she shot upward through the whirling current.

Popping up out of the water, she gasped and choked desperately for air. The current dragged her away from the rock, and seconds later, she was bobbing like a cork down the angry Colorado.

Time crawled by. Kendra's eyes were burning with silt, and everything was a blur. The river carried her along with frightening speed. Automatically, she assumed the safest position for riding through rapids: lying on her back, facing downstream, her feet raised to protect her head and organs from being smashed against the rocks.

Kendra knew she was going into shock. The thought of her sister drowning, and perhaps Nolan, as well, devastated her. How many lives were going to be taken today? Floundering weakly and dodging boulders, she finally made it to a gravel bar. Coughing up river water, she managed to crawl toward solid ground, collapsing half on land, half in the water.

Gratefully, she dug her fingers into the warm sand. She was safe! But what about Debby and Nolan?

Eventually, Kendra found the strength to crawl out of the numbing water. Sitting up, she wiped at her eyes, but her hands were caked with sand. Finally, her tears washed her eyes out and she was able to look around blearily. The thundering of the rapids was constant, but she hardly heard it now.

Looking upstream, Kendra spotted the huge red boulder that had been their undoing. There was no sign of anyone nearby. And then she spied Nolan, fighting his way around it. Somehow, he had gotten back up there; how, Kendra didn't know. Nolan was alive.

But where was Debby? Where was her baby sister? Struggling to stand up, Kendra staggered, with fatigue. Cupping her hands, she screamed, "Debby? Debby? Where *are* you?"

Frantically, she scanned the river. She could see where the rapids smoothed out below, but there was no Debby. A horrible feeling encased Kendra. She sank to her knees, covered her eyes and sobbed. In her heart, she knew her sister was dead. She'd gotten sucked into the whirlpool, never to surface again. Her body could still be down there, going around and around....

The thought was nauseating. Lifting her head, Kendra looked back at the murderous rock, and her heart slammed into her chest. Nolan was there, lifting Debby out of the water! Somehow, he had found her sister! With a cry, Kendra staggered toward the edge of the gravel bar. She saw Nolan grip Debby in a safety carry and shove off the rock. He headed straight to where she was standing, a good quarter mile downriver.

Tears scalded Kendra's cheeks as she waited. She saw Nolan's pale face, the blood still dripping from the gash on his forehead. Debby was listless in his grasp as he kept her head above water and maneuvered toward the sandbar. The color of her sister's face frightened Kendra. It was blue-gray, indicating she wasn't breathing.

Sloshing out into the river, Kendra was knee deep when Nolan reached out to grab her hand. Gripping him, she hauled him and Debby into the shallows. He was gasping and sobbing for breath, her gaze centered on Debby, whose eyes were open and staring sightlessly.

"No!" Kendra screamed. She grabbed her sister's life vest and hauled her out of the water, laying her sister down. Nolan crawled out and came to her side, and together, they tried to revive her.

How long Kendra gave CPR to Debby, she didn't know. Nolan had rolled her over on her stomach and pushed a lot of water out of her lungs. And then they'd laid her on her back and begun the procedure. They worked tirelessly, without words, for an hour, until their own physical reserves deserted them.

"I—it's no use...." Nolan croaked at last. "I—

I'm sorry…so sorry. She's dead, Kendra. Oh, God, I'm so sorry…."

"No!" Kendra screamed. Her arms were so tired they shook. The adrenaline had left her, and she was exhausted. But, glaring at Nolan, she snarled, "Keep working! Help me! We can save her!"

Though physically spent, Nolan tried. But finally he looked up, his eyes burning with tears. "It's been over an hour, Kendra. I'm sorry…Debby is dead…."

Suddenly, Kendra gave out. She fell to the sand, her cheek against the gritty surface. Her entire body trembled, and she was too weak to fight anymore. Crying out her sister's name, she shut her eyes and heard terrible sounds coming from her throat. Within two years, she had lost all her family, except for her grandmother Hattie, who lived in California. Kendra didn't want to believe Nolan. If only she was strong enough, she could keep doing CPR, and Debby would live!

But then the world grew gray, and Kendra felt darkness swamping her just as the Colorado's current had. As she surrendered to the darkness, a palpable rage surged up through her dimming consciousness. This was all Nolan's fault! He'd said he knew the river. He'd said he was an expert. And he'd let Debby die. The bastard had killed her sister, the last of her family. As Kendra spiraled down into a whirlpool of grief, whatever love she had had for Nolan was destroyed.

Fondness turned to hatred in that cataclysmic

moment. Grief and distrust replaced her confidence and belief him. As the last shreds of consciousness left her, Kendra vowed she'd never love him again.

Chapter 1

"Is everything all right, Kendra?" Calen Hernandez asked as she peeked around the open door of the guest room. The woman was tall, with sleek black hair pulled back into a ponytail. Kendra admired her colorful yellow breeches and fuscia T-shirt.

Having just arrived in Quito and being beyond exhausted, Kendra smiled when she saw Calen holding two cups of coffee. "You are a goddess," she declared. Taking one colorful mug, she gestured for Calen to sit down at the desk opposite the large bed. "Thank you." Kendra was glad she wore her jungle clothing of green nylon trousers and a white sleeveless tank top.

Chuckling, her hostess said, "I've been called many things in my life, but never a goddess. I kind of like that label. I think I'll keep it."

Kendra sat on the edge of the queen-size bed and rested the mug on her knee. She'd had a long trip, and it was about to get more difficult.

"You seem concerned about something," Calen noted, sipping her coffee. "Did I come at a bad time?"

"Not at all." Kendra took a sip in turn, mulling over what she should say. She stared down at her pair of sensible brown shoes. "When I found out from your husband that Professor Nolan Galloway had been invited to hear your proposal on locating a section of the Emerald Key necklace, I almost backed out of the project."

Tilting her head, Calen asked, "Why, Kendra?"

"There was—an incident many years ago. I can't forget it. Or…forgive him."

Frowning, Calen said, "As owners of the Vesica Piscis Foundation, we did a lot of research on who should retrieve the next emerald sphere from the necklace. Every authority said you and Professor Nolan were the best."

"I'm not surprised. We've both become experts on gender issues and women's rightful place in society," Kendra professed with a sigh. She wasn't sure she wanted to discuss her history with Nolan, but she'd liked Calen from the moment she'd met her. The warmth between them reminded her poignantly of her bond with her younger sister. Debby's loss still felt like a sharp stick gouging her grieving heart.

"Our research showed that you two were engaged to be married a long time ago," Calen cautiously ventured. She crossed her legs. "I don't mean to pry, but can you tell me a little about what happened?"

Compressing her lips, Kendra stared down at the cup she held between her hands. It was midday, nearly eighty degrees with the sky cloudy. Odd that a hot cup of coffee would feel so comforting in the high humidity and temperature, but it did. "I guess as the organizer of the expedition, you have a right to know the story, but I'd rather not publicize it too much," Kendra said.

"Whatever you say stays with us. It's not going into a database. We just need to understand the uncomfortable dynamic between you and Professor Nolan. Maybe we can somehow change it. We want this mission to be as easy as possible on everyone."

Kendra nodded. "Okay, the bottom line is that Nolan caused the death of my only sister. We'd lost our parents in an auto accident on the Navajo reservation two years earlier. Debby was my only sibling."

"When we did background research on you, Kendra, we became aware of the tragedy. I'm so sorry." Calen rubbed her furrowed brow. "How awful. I lost my parents when I was very young, too.

I saw them murdered by guards at the Santa Maria emerald mine. I know how you must feel about the loss of your parents."

That piece of knowledge forged a powerful link between Kendra and this woman. "I didn't know, Calen. I'm very sorry."

"It was a long time ago. The pain is always there in the background, but it's manageable now. I'll always love and miss them. Time has helped blunt the grief, but it will never, ever go away."

"You're right about that," Kendra said quietly. She sipped more of the rich coffee. Shafts of sunlight slanted in the floor-to-ceiling windows, reminding her symbolically of hope from a higher source.

"You said Professor Galloway caused the death of your sister? How did it happen? Were you there?"

Kendra girded herself internally. She owed Calen Hernandez an explanation about why she didn't want to work with Galloway. Yet the lure of finding part of the mystical Emerald Key necklace was too great to resist. Kendra had to take on the mission. As an archaeologist, she considered the assignment akin to going after the Holy Grail. And she couldn't say no, even if it involved the man she hated more than anyone in the world.

"This will take a few minutes to tell," she warned.

Calen shrugged. "I've got all the time in the world. Professor Galloway isn't going to arrive for another two hours. Tell me what happened, Kendra."

* * *

Nolan Galloway was placing his bags in his first-floor guest room at the condo when his host, Reno Manchahi, appeared in the doorway.

After introductions, Reno asked, "You ready for our meeting, Professor?"

Straightening, Nolan looked over at the Native American. Reno was a large, hard-muscled Apache warrior, and it showed in every line of his copper-colored face. He wore his straight black hair long and loose across his broad shoulders. This was one dangerous dude, with a military bearing. What was he doing on a project like the Emerald Key?

Nolan had a lot of questions, but decided to table them for now. He was sure the mission planning session would reveal everything.

"Yes, I'm ready. I'll just grab my trusty yellow legal pad and pen," Nolan said, retrieving the items before following Manchahi out of the room and down the hall. He wore a green polo shirt beneath his canvas vest.

His gut was twisting like a ball of snakes. Now thirty-five, he should be over losing Kendra Johnson's sister in the raging Colorado River nearly a decade earlier. He wiped his hand down the side of his ivory dockers. Knowing that Kendra was invited to be part of the team, he questioned his own ability to remain objective and not get hooked into the hatred he knew she still carried for him. She blamed him for the loss of her sister; he'd known that from the moment Debby lay lifeless on that sandbar. He had been young then and had immediately accepted the blame. It had been his fault, but there were extenuating circumstances that helped cause the accident. Kendra hadn't wanted to know that.

As he followed Reno down the highly polished mahogany hall, Nolan tried to suppress his old feelings for Kendra. He'd loved her so much. More than life. He'd nearly *given* his life to rescue her that day, when she'd been pinned against that rock in the whirlpool. She'd never known about his last-ditch attempts to save Debby.

Nolan's conscience smarted. He had anger of his own to deal with, over Kendra's unfair rage toward him. Whatever trust he had forged with her during their relationship had shattered on that terrible day. Trust was not in the cards then, and he was fairly sure it wouldn't be now. But he would see.

As they entered a room filled with blueprints, Nolan realized this was where the Vesica Piscis Foundation was being temporarily headquartered. From the large windows, he could see the ongoing construction of the massive ten-story building about a mile from the condo. It was impressive. And so was their mission. His mood rocked back and forth between the giddy realization that he was being asked to find a sphere from the Emerald Key necklace, and the fact of having to do it with Kendra Johnson, who hated him.

Wiping the sweat from his upper lip, Nolan turned and followed Reno down yet another hall. Somehow, he had to keep his personal feelings out of this. Archaeology was in his blood, and to know that two of the emerald spheres were already in Reno and Calen's possession was mind-blowing to him. These people knew how to find them, no doubt. And being on the team to locate a third one made Nolan salivate as no other project would. No, this mission could be the crowning event in his career as an archaeologist, and give his alma mater, Princeton, world fame. Nolan knew he'd have to share the glory with Kendra and Harvard University, but that didn't bother him. Princeton would get equal billing and that's all he cared about.

They turned into a large room on the right, and Nolan took a deep breath to gird himself. As he entered, he saw a large planning table in the center, covered with papers and documents and flanked by four wooden stools. And at one end stood Kendra Johnson, glaring at him, her haunting green eyes filled with rage.

He felt his own anger rising, but he couldn't tear his gaze from her. It had been nine years since he'd last seen her. He'd purposely avoided lectures and workshops she'd attend. Nolan hadn't wanted to be anywhere near her. But now, here she was. Her Navajo face, oval with high cheekbones and all those Irish freckles, and framed by that glorious red hair, was nearly his undoing. She looked so young and vibrant. Vital. Beautiful. And Nolan could feel her hatred oozing over him as he approached the large table.

Reno introduced his wife to Nolan. Calen smiled and shook his hand with genuine warmth and welcome, and he felt the quiet strength of the woman. He'd done quite a bit of research on her, Reno and their newly formed nonprofit organization, Vesica Piscis. He knew she was a billionaire oil baroness, with many producing wells just off the coast of Ecuador.

Reno reintroduced Kendra to Nolan.

"Dr. Johnson," Nolan said, his voice gruff. "It's a pleasure to be working with you on this project." That was a lie, but he had to be civilized and diplomatic—two things he wrestled with constantly. His Irish temperament always got him into trouble. His grandfather Otis, who had lived on the reservation in Cherokee, North Carolina, always told him to say little and listen a lot. Nolan constantly worked to develop that habit.

"Professor Galloway," Kendra replied coolly. She sat on a four-legged stool at the table.

"Have a seat, Professor," Calen invited, and she gestured to the opposite end.

Glad to be as far away as he could get from Kendra's glare, he nodded and complied. Nolan set his pad on the table, noticing that there was a map and a red file folder at each place. His curiosity warred with his emotional reactions to seeing

Kendra. Her beauty was in full bloom, now that she was in her early thirties. Trying not to eye those provocative full lips of hers, now a compressed line, Nolan couldn't help but remember how soft and pliant they'd been when the two of them made love. His body heated up, reminding him all too eloquently of the part of him that still desired her. Dismayed at his unexpected reaction, Nolan focused on Reno, who sat down opposite his wife at the table.

"We're glad you're both able to be here," Reno told them. "If you'll open the file in front of you, we'll get on with the mission to locate the next emerald sphere."

Nolan's eyes widened when he opened his folder. "This…this is what we're looking for?" He lifted the glossy color photo and stared at it with awe. The emerald sphere sat on a black velvet pillow. He could read the word carved on it: *Forgiveness.* Glancing up, he noticed Kendra's mouth had dropped open, too, as she gazed at the photo in her own packet. As an archaeologist, Nolan had heard the legend about the mysterious missing necklace, said to be able to heal or destroy the world, depending upon who got their hands on it.

He set down the photo. "This is real?"

"Yes," Calen said. She told the story of how she and Reno had found the first sphere in a cave here in Ecuador. And then she shared that their other teammates, Ana and Mace Ridfort, presently at the

Village of the Clouds in Peru receiving metaphysical training, had found the second sphere near Machu Picchu, the sacred mountain stronghold of the Incan emperor *Pachacuti.*

"Now," Reno told them, when Calen had finished, "we have a lead on where the third sphere might be located." He pulled a map and a photo from his pack and laid them on the table. "Take a look."

Nolan could barely put aside the photos of the two spheres. All he wanted to do was study them, absorb them. His heart beat with excitement until he looked across the table and once again saw the rage banked in Kendra's eyes—aimed at him. Obviously, she wanted to make it clear she had neither forgotten nor forgiven him. His own anger flared. No way would she listen to his side. How could love turn to such hatred?

Nolan knew how. He'd created the situation, and there was nothing he could do to bring Kendra's beloved sister back to her.

Drawing a calming breath, he glanced at the map. "This is Southwestern England," he said in surprise.

"And what is this photo of?" Kendra asked, pointing to it.

Calen smiled. "You're both going to realize that the Vesica Piscis Foundation is more than just your average nonprofit group."

She pointed to Reno and then herself. "We're mystics trained in the paranormal or metaphysical world. I know this isn't something most archaeologists think about or embrace, but if you're working as a team to find this next sphere, you need to believe what I'm about to say." Her tone turned serious. "If you don't, then you can't undertake this mission. It's that simple."

Nolan hesitated. "Paranormal?"

"Let me tell you about my skills," Calen said. "I'm a shape-shifter by heritage. I can change from my human form if I choose, into that of a jaguar." She looked at Reno. "My husband can do the same thing."

Nolan blinked, thoughtfully assimilating her words. "I'm familiar with indigenous cultures having legends and rituals involving shape-shifting. I've just never met anyone who admitted they had that skill." He studied Calen with fresh curiosity.

"Professor Nolan," Kendra said stiffly, "mysticism was part and parcel of every culture in the ancient world. You know that." There was an edge of anger in her husky voice.

Stung, Nolan stared across the table at his ex-fiancée. He knew that on a personal level she embraced the Navajo belief system. Even though her father had been a world-famous archaeologist from Ireland, the only things she seemed to have inherited from him were his famous temper, his love of the past and his freckles. "I'm not saying I don't believe Calen, Dr. Johnson."

Reno cleared his throat. "This isn't up for debate.

It's a fact." He glanced at the two sparring archaeologists. "And we want to know what paranormal talent each of you possesses. You both have a Vesica Piscis birthmark on the back of your neck, as we do. It is a symbol for right actions. And its presence also guarantees you have some paranormal skill."

Calen looked at Kendra. "You come from Native American roots, and so does Professor Galloway. Reno is Apache. We know that, genetically, paranormal skills filter down from one generation to another. So, Kendra, what is your skill?"

Taken off guard, Kendra hesitated. "Uh, well…" Above all, she didn't want Galloway to make fun of her. He'd hurt her enough already. Lifting her head, she glared at him. "If I divulge this information, I want assurance it will go no farther than this room. I have an academic reputation to protect."

Struggling with his temper, Nolan returned her glare. "I want the same assurance from you, Doctor."

"You have my word," she grated.

He nodded. "And you have mine."

"Not that your word is worth anything," Kendra growled. "You'll sign a statement to that effect right now or this discussion is done."

Frustration thrummed through Nolan. Kendra was prickly as hell about her standing in the archaeological community. She always had been. He quickly scribbled out a promise, signed and dated it. Pushing it across the table, he snarled, "Is this good enough, Dr. Johnson?"

Glancing at it, she nodded. "It will do."

"I want the same from you, Doctor."

Kendra quickly wrote out a similar statement, then tossed it at Nolan, whose blue eyes were burning. "There you go, Professor. Trust isn't our gig, is it? You never could be trusted, then or now."

"Please," Calen said quietly, looking from one to the other, "can we declare a truce and get on with the things that are really important?"

Swallowing hard, Nolan said, "Of course. I believe Dr. Johnson was going to reveal her mystical gift to all of us."

How she wanted to curse at him! But Kendra swallowed the words. Instead, she directed her attention to Calen and Reno. "My mother possessed a gift called psychometry." Gesturing with her hands, she said, "If I touch something, I pick up a vibe. Sometimes I feel heat or cold. Other times, I see a face, or I literally see what appears to be color movie footage of a scene. When I pick up an old shard at a dig and concentrate on it, I know who the maker was and what the pot was used for. I also know its approximate age."

"That's wonderful," Calen said with awe.

"So you can touch a tree, and find out who also touched it?" Reno demanded.

Nodding, Kendra risked a quick look at Nolan,

who seemed completely surprised. She'd never divulged this to anyone, for fear her archaeology career would go up in flames. "That's right. I'm like a bird dog on a scent, except that I don't smell it. I touch something and then get a little—or a lot—of information regarding it."

Nolan stared at her. "That's why your articles are so rich with details and possibilities when you write about discoveries at your digs. I always wondered how you could know such things."

Squirming uncomfortably, Kendra warned him in a low voice, "Yes, that's right, Professor. And you'll have to remember our agreement."

"I will," Nolan said abruptly. But his mind swam with the implications of her mystical talent. It was stunning. A gift that could open up the annals of archaeology and solve a lot of mysteries. And then he realized how careful Kendra had to be. All too aware that many of their colleagues didn't believe in mysticism, Nolan understood her fear of having her abilities made public. He could, quite literally, destroy her entire career. But that was something he'd never do, despite her doubt.

"And what about *your* gift, Professor?" Reno asked.

Shrugging, he said, "I've got telekinesis abilities through my Cherokee side. Grandfather Otis, who trained me when I was a kid, also possessed it."

"Show us," Kendra said, bewildered that he'd never divulged this paranormal gift to her. Why hadn't he?

Nolan saw a pencil lying halfway between them on the table.

"Watch…." He pointed his index finger. As he concentrated, the pencil began to roll toward Kendra.

Gasping, she leaped off the stool and backed away. The pencil continued to roll toward her until it tottered on the edge of the table.

And then Nolan willed it back, toward the center of the table, where he stopped it. He clasped his hands on the table and looked at all of them. "As you see, I have the ability to move objects, or to push or pull myself in the direction I want. I've always had this skill. My grandfather, rest his soul, helped me understand it, tame it, focus it. He taught me the morals and values of when and how to use this power."

"Why didn't you tell me?" Kendra demanded, holding his gaze.

"I didn't feel it was important, and it sure wasn't going to be received with open arms by the archaeology community. I just decided to say nothing."

Kendra came back to the table, shaken what she'd seen. She sat down and gawked at the pencil on the table. "How do you use it?"

He released a ragged sigh. It took everything he had to look Kendra in the eye. "Remember after the raft plowed into that rock in the Colorado River?"

Stunned, she stared at him. His face was alive with pain from the past, his turquoise eyes narrowed and dark. "I— Yes…"

"I was thrown out of the raft, and the current dragged me downstream, away from you."

"That's right," she whispered, her voice choking with sudden emotion. "I remember that."

Shaking his head, Nolan rasped, "Did you ever wonder how I was able to get back to that rock where Debby was trapped and pull her out of the whirlpool?"

Stared at him, her eyes wide. "No…"

"I know you didn't," he told her quietly. "I used my telekinesis to do it, despite the strong current." He held up his right hand. "My power has limits. It takes life energy to move anything, or pull something to me, or me to it. I expended my entire store of energy getting back to you, to the rock and Debby. I pulled your sister out of the whirlpool with my powers, but it was too late. I couldn't save her. But I was able to save you…."

Chapter 2

Kendra felt her world shatter as she heard Nolan's whispered, raw statement. For the moment, she was at a loss for words. All she saw was the pain, the guilt and longing in his large, intelligent eyes. The emotions sent a riffle of heat through the cracks in her heart. The hatred she felt for him never went away completely; it had ebbed and flowed like a tide over the years after losing Debby. Now, Kendra's heart was aching with a new sensation: of wanting Nolan as she had before the accident occurred.

Shaken, she tried to fight these sudden feelings. She knew the truth now. While she hadn't been able to find her sister in that whirlpool, Nolan had. He had pulled Debby out of the perilous waters, had tried to save her.

"Let's just stick to this mission, shall we?" Kendra muttered, looking to their hostess.

"Of course." Calen nodded. She pointed to the file folder in front of Kendra. "If you'll both go to page four, you'll see a drawing I made from a vision I had a few days ago."

Glad to be occupied with the business at hand, Kendra pulled out the simple ink drawing, focusing on it and trying to ignore Nolan's larger-than-life presence. "These look like two earphones, or headsets, one smaller than the other," she said. Inside them were other half circles, reminding her of ripples produced when a pebble was tossed into the still waters of a pond. "This was shown to you in your dream?"

"Yes. I have more than one paranormal skill in place." Calen grinned. "I have precognitive dreams about future events. When I had this vision, I saw a windmill, too. Our other team member, Mason Ridfort, who has knowledge of crop circles, said there is a place near Wiltshire, England, known as Windmill Hill. He said this hill contains the remains of a Neolithic fort. Around it are farmers' fields. He feels this crop circle will appear near Windmill Hill."

"Crop circles," Nolan muttered. "I've been studying them for years." He avoided looking at Kendra, and instead glanced toward Calen. "No one knows how or why they appear. But I'm fascinated with their evolving symbology."

"So am I," Kendra said. "These half circles mean something."

"If you were able to stand in them, Kendra, could you use your psychometry skills to find out what they are all about?" Reno asked.

"I don't know. I've never really tried to use my talent on a crop circle."

"If you can hold something in your hands and get information off it," Nolan said, "then you should be able to stand in a place and get info, too. It's only logical."

Kendra wanted to be angry at his presumption, but somehow, the feeling wasn't there. What was going on? She was suffering from jet lag and stressed out because she had to be near him once more. "This is an ink drawing. Of a dream."

Calen nodded. "Yes, but my precogs come true, Kendra. Reno and I feel you two need to fly to London, rent a car and drive to Windmill Hill."

"And this has to do with finding the next emerald sphere?" Nolan demanded.

"Yes," Calen said, "it's the beginning of a road map, if you will. Projected by the emerald sphere, to show us where it's located."

"We know the spirit of that sphere is in touch with Calen," Reno murmured. "What we want to do is transfer this communication process to you." He looked at the archaeologists. "We feel if you go to Windmill Hill, pitch a tent and wait, the creator of these crop circles will come and carve this into one of the fields around the hill. When it happens, you're to go down to it." Reno gazed at Kendra. "And I think if you step into it, you'll get the next piece of information needed to find the sphere."

"That seems possible," Kendra said hesitantly. "But I feel wobbly on this, Reno. I've only used my psychometry on shards and implements at my digs."

"You can do it," Nolan stated. "You've always been very intuitive."

While she wanted to accept his praise, Kendra fought it. "I can try," she murmured, "with no promises."

"Of course," Calen said, reaching out and touching Kendra's arm. "I'm sure this is all terribly new to you, but it's where we have to go in order to locate the next sphere." With a slight smile, she added, "It's kind of like a treasure hunt, where you go from one clue to the next. We don't know why the spirit of a sphere leads us on like this. Maybe it's a game to them. Or maybe it's to ensure we are serious about finding it. This could be a test of our resolve."

"What we do know," Reno told them, "is that the spirit of each sphere has talked with us. We are of the Light, the *Taqe,* and this necklace wants to be with us. We're charged with finding the spheres and putting the necklace back together. Once that's done,

Ana will wear it. Ana Elena Rafael is part of our team here, and Mason Ridfort's wife."

"Ana is the woman of the Inca legends," Calen stated solemnly. "It is said that if she wears the fully assembled necklace, the *Taqe* will have a chance to bring peace to Earth for a thousand years. We think this is a worthy cause to work for. And we hope you agree."

"A thousand years of peace," Nolan exclaimed, looking around the large, sunny room. "Who doesn't want that?"

Grimly, Reno said, "Good question. We have to warn you that if you two decide to work on this mission, there's danger involved. It won't necessarily be seen. Usually, it's invisible, and can manifest at any time and in any form."

Frowning, Kendra asked, "What are you talking about? Are other universities sending archaeological teams after this sphere, too?"

"No," Calen said. "We have enemies, the *Tupay*, or heavy energy people. They tend to embody all the negative aspects of human beings, Kendra. A person who is greedy, who wants power, who will murder, lie, cheat or steal, is often of the *Tupay*."

"Plus we have an immortal enemy, a master sorcerer by the name of Victor Carancho Guerra, who is after the Emerald Key just like we are," Reno told them. "He's at least four thousand years old. He stays alive by taking over the body of a young person as the body he's been inhabiting dies."

"Guerra has special powers," he added. "He can possess anything—human, animal, insect…you name it. When he takes over a human, they can't fight him off. He inhabits their body and controls their will. Not only does he have their physical form as his vehicle, but he adopts the personality of his host. Guerra can draw on a wealth of memories and knowledge. With his immense power, he can locate you, tail you, and very likely steal the sphere if you find it."

"If Guerra manages to steal it," Calen interjected, "he will take it to the Other Worlds, the invisible dimensions around us, and keep it. We're at war with him and his legions to get the necklace."

She sighed. "Whoever assembles the seven spheres and wears the necklace will have ultimate power here on Earth. If Guerra gets to it before we can, there will be a thousand more years of the chaos and war we have now." She cut them each a grim look. "Which is why we're so eager to locate the spheres."

"Phew, that's some story," Nolan declared. "I'm into symbols, not ghosts and goblins," he joked, trying to relieve the tension in the room.

Calen chuckled. "I understand your reaction. Reno and I live with the paranormal world every day, but most people do not. We understand you and Kendra might not be used to all this, but taking on this mission, you're going to be dumped into it and all its dangers. We can't, in good conscience, not tell you about Guerra and his *Tupay* forces. We know he will go after you, follow you and do all he can to get that next sphere."

"I've heard of possession through my mother, who was Navajo," Kendra said. "Our people believe in spirits, some of whom can be harmful to human beings."

"That's right, they can be," Reno agreed. "Most indigenous people accept that some unhappy spirits wander around the planet, for many reasons. But they aren't your concern. Guerra is. When he possesses a person and then exits their body when he's done using it, the host dies instantly."

The words slammed into Kendra, and she glanced across the table at Nolan. His expression was grim. She then turned to Reno. "So how do we protect ourselves?"

"You can't. He's that powerful."

A cold chill worked through her.

"But listen," Calen urged, "Guerra wants you alive, not dead. Chances are he'll take over other peoples' bodies, not yours. He wants you to lead him to the sphere. If you're dead, you can't do that. So he'll inhabit individuals around you, and that's what you have to stay alert for. Some people may not be who they seem to be. They can't fight Guerra's power. And they'll have no way to communicate to you that he has control of them."

Reno held Kendra's worried gaze. "There is one way to resist Guerra's control, and that's with your heart. If you can project your love toward him, he can't harm you."

"Easier said than done," Kendra muttered. "I'd have a tough time loving someone who wants to kill me."

"It isn't easy," Calen agreed quietly, "but that is what the *Taqe,* the people of the Light, are charged with trying to do, Kendra. We have to rise into our heart level, tap into our compassion, and love them despite the monsters they have become."

"It's the ultimate test," Reno said, giving his wife a warm look. "And if you go after a sphere, that's where your challenge will be—learning to love and forgive."

Kendra grimaced. Those words could easily include Nolan, and how she felt about him killing her sister. "So, if I'm hearing you correctly, you think Guerra will tail us?"

"Yes. That's what he's done in the past. He won't strike until he knows where the emerald sphere is located."

"And when he strikes?" Nolan asked.

"Do what you can to protect yourselves," Reno said. "We're dealing with the invisible realms. You can't take a gun and shoot Guerra, for bullets pass harmlessly through spirit. Ana had a run-in with the sorcerer and she used love from her heart to force him to leave Mace alone. And it worked."

"The heart…" Kendra looked down and murmured, "Something so simple, and yet so hard to do. Love your enemy, quite literally."

"That's right," Calen said. "Ground zero. The heart versus the lower passions in people—that's where we're at in this world. You can see it playing out on every level."

"Our heart becomes our protection," Nolan said with a tender glance at Kendra. He wanted so badly to dissolve the barriers between them. Her green eyes were dark with worry. The same worry he'd seen that fateful day on the raft. "I view this as an opportunity to grow. Maybe we can both work with our hearts, Kendra, and something good will come out of this mission."

When Nolan whispered her name, Kendra felt a riffle of warmth flow across her. This was the man she'd fallen in love with so long ago. This was the feeling she'd fought ever since. But here it was again. Steeling herself to resist the plea she saw in the depths of his eyes, she replied, "I'm not going to focus on that. What I will focus on is finding that sphere. My university wants it and so do I."

Spoken like a true archaeologist. Nolan didn't say that out loud. An acidic comment would only have inflamed the tenuous situation. Okay, so Kendra was letting him know the status quo would remain between them. Deep down, he felt tired. Tired of being angry and upset for nearly a decade. A part of him wanted to call a truce, but the stubborn look on Kendra's face warned him off. Sighing, Nolan said, "I feel the same way."

"Good," Calen said. "Now we want you to look at my drawing. Do either of you sense anything? What could this symbol mean?"

Glad to focus on something other than Nolan, Kendra looked down at the paper. "It reminds me of the old saying, 'As above, so below,' because the two images are exactly the same except one is smaller than the other."

"A reflection of something," Reno said, nodding. "There is a dualism here. They also look like two round breasts, one a bit larger than the other with half circles."

"Exactly," Nolan interjected. "This could be the breasts of the Great Mother Goddess. Or could represent women and the divine feminine. That would indicate that a woman should go into that crop circle, not a man. Don't forget, milk comes from a woman's breast, providing sustenance, and life itself. Perhaps the creator of this symbol is a woman. It also looks like a whirlpool of some sort." He didn't like saying so, but that's what the drawing made him think of— the whirlpool that had taken Debby's life. Nolan found bitter synchronicity between the symbol and their own lives.

Smarting when Nolan said that word, Kendra felt rage bubbling up in her. She clenched her teeth, then forced herself to take a breath. "Why don't we examine at these from an astronomical perspective?" she said. "If you look at NASA photos of deep space taken through the Hubble telescope, you'll see wormholes. This reminds me of a wormhole, a tube or tunnel to get from one point in time and space to another. That would fit with 'As above, so below.'"

"Oh!" Calen cried, "That's an incredible connection! That would make a lot of sense, Kendra. From a paranormal view, wormholes are a way to travel from one dimension to another, transit point from one to the next."

Reno grinned at Kendra. "Your insights are fantastic. I agree with my wife. The fact the two circles are touching must mean they are connected. And each has a whirlpool of semicircles within each and give us a sense of being pulled or drawn to it, just as if we were in a real whirlpool, we'd get sucked down into it. This drawing is creating that same kind of feeling for me. And how to get from one to the next is through a tunnel, or channel of some kind. The wormhole theory. Brilliant."

Nolan nodded. "This makes a lot of sense to me as a scientist," he agreed, admiration for her evident in his glance. "If this symbol appears in one of those fields below Windmill Hill, does it mean that stepping into it will take you to another dimension?"

Kendra met his probing gaze. "I don't know. I've never dealt with a crop circle before. I guess if this symbol pops up in a farm field, I'll find out, won't I?"

Hearing the anger carefully disguised in her husky voice, Nolan erected his own barriers to stop her from tearing another pound of flesh out of his aching heart. He noticed she said "I" and not "we," which meant she hadn't quite accepted him as part of the team on this mission. What did he expect? Kendra saw this as an adventure, with Harvard getting the lion's share of credit. The archaeologist from Princeton in him wanted to argue, but Nolan opted to put it aside. He had to, because finding the sphere meant hope for a better future for all mankind. That was far more important than squabbling.

Calen broke the silence. "I think we have the mission clarified. There's a plane leaving Quito for London tonight. You'll fly first class, my secretary has all your papers in order. There will be a rental car waiting for you when you land. And she's made a reservation near Chalice Well in Glastonbury, where you will stay. From there, you can drive into Wiltshire county, which is about forty-five minutes away. You'll set up camp on top of Windmill Hill, then wait and see if this crop circle appears."

"Sounds good to me," Nolan said, rubbing his hands together and smiling at the group. "I'm ready for this adventure."

Kendra frowned. She didn't like the idea of having to sit next to Nolan on the flight. It was a childish reaction, but that's how she felt. She could see excitement gleaming in his blue eyes. Nolan lived for the hunt. He was well-known in archaeological circles to be an aggressive bloodhound once on a scent. And he was finding new discoveries all the time. They were the right team for this mission, she reluctantly admitted.

As she glanced down at her clasped hands, she knew her struggle *would* be with her heart, with her unresolved rage at Nolan. She hadn't been able to forgive him. And in the morass was a part of her that yearned to love him once more. Suddenly, she felt like an emotional mess, the last person who should go on this mission. But the archaeologist in her, the ardent professional, had to rise above her personal feelings and find this sphere—for the right reasons. Added to the mix was a sorcerer who could possess and kill a person at will. Who was the greater threat here? Nolan or Guerra? Right now, Kendra wasn't sure.

Tapping the drawing, Nolan wondered aloud, "If Kendra steps into this circle, once it appears, do you have any ideas where it might take her?"

Shrugging his broad shoulders, Reno said, "I don't have a clue. Calen?"

"Me, either, Nolan." She looked at Kendra. "I guess the best that can be said is that you'll go on an adventure into the unknown."

"What if it takes her to Guerra?" Nolan pressed.

Sighing, Calen murmured, "I'm not sure of anything, except that you must combat the sorcerer with your heart, your goodness and love. It's true he lives in the Other Worlds, but I have a strong sixth sense that whoever is creating these crop circles on Earth is not *Tupay*. I feel that they are *Taqe*, of the Light. If Kendra does step into one, I don't believe it will send her to Guerra."

"It's just a hunch, though," Nolan said.

"The best I've got. Yes."

Worried, Nolan held Kendra's flat green stare. He was far more intuitive than he ever let anyone know and he could feel her wrestling with a lot of emotions right now. Most of them aimed at him—and their painful past. "What if she disappears?" He glanced over at their hosts.

"I don't know," Calen hesitantly admitted. "There's a lot about this mission we aren't sure of, Nolan. I wish we were."

"Don't worry about me." Kendra snapped and glared over at Nolan. "You take care of yourself on this little jaunt and the rest will take care of itself."

Nodding, he replied, "Okay."

"Is there anything else, Calen?" Kendra demanded tightly.

"No, we've covered it." She gave each of them another file. "There's info here on crop circles, the area around Glastonbury and the archaeology of the region. You can peruse this material on the flight to London."

Gripping her file, Kendra stood. "Thank you for this. Now, if you'll excuse me, I'm going to grab a nap. Would you wake me two hours before we leave?"

"Of course," Calen said.

Nolan watched as Kendra quickly exited the

room. He risked a glance at the husband-and-wife team. "Things are a little tense between us," he said apologetcially. "I think once we focus on finding the sphere, conditions will chill out."

Reno nodded. "We understand there's a lot of bitterness between the two of you, but we're hoping you can work beyond that for the greater good here, Nolan."

"I plan to," he promised, as he picked up his second file folder. Sliding off the stool, he shrugged. "Who knows? Maybe this trip is exactly what we need."

Calen ran her fingers through her dark, shoulder-length hair, then got up and walked around to the table where Reno was sitting. Sliding her arm around his shoulders, she said, "Nolan, this mission can't be a solo operation. It's going to require both of you working as a team."

Reno wrapped an arm around Calen's waist. "If you two are distracted by one another and your unhappy past, you aren't going to be alert to Guerra. You seem to be less affected by the personal tension, Nolan. It's going to be up to you to keep Kendra out of trouble with that sorcerer."

Nolan quirked his mouth as he met the couple's worried gazes. "I'm very aware of the life-and-death dance we're entering into here. Kendra might not be, and that leaves her open to attack."

"Precisely," Calen glumly agreed. "You have two jobs, Nolan. One is to assist Kendra and the other is to keep watch."

Nolan's heart contracted with fear for Kendra, not for himself. Wanting to ease the couple's worry, he halted at the open door. "I'll do my best. For the rest of the day, I'm going to do a little walking around your estate, if you don't mind."

"Go right ahead," Reno told him. "Maybe some fresh air will help."

Nolan thanked them for their generous hospitality and left. He walked back to his bedroom and deposited the files in his worn canvas briefcase, which he'd had since he became an archaeologist. He'd bought it shortly after losing his other one in the rafting incident on the Colorado.

Grabbing his baseball cap, he headed down the hall. And now he had to work with Kendra, when she wanted nothing to do with him. Plus he had to protect her from a sorcerer who would stalk their every move. As he opened the door to the manicured rose garden, Nolan tried to quell the churning feelings in his gut. This mission had incredible meaning on so many levels. And yet it hinged on two people who didn't want to work together.

"There are no accidents," he murmured to himself. "Not ever."

Chapter 3

"My lord," Publius Hadrian said, "you called me?"

Victor Carancho Guerra sat at his desk in the Dark Castle in the Other Worlds. "I did, Sir Hadrian. Sit down, please." He gestured to the straight-backed wooden chair in front of his desk. As master sorcerer of the *Tupay*, Victor was in charge not only of his massive army in spirit, but also those in human form. Hadrian was such a man—his finest, most loyal warrior in their order of Dark Knights, an elite group of men and women who lived to serve him.

Victor was now in spirit, having had his body taken away from him by Mace Ridfort, a Warrior for the Light, his immortal, ageless enemy. That didn't stop him from amassing his *Tupay* army, however, and Victor was just getting up to speed to go after the emerald spheres. Once all seven were in his hands, he could assemble the powerful Emerald Key necklace, wear it and become the ruler of Earth, once and for all. For thousands of years, Victor had kept his focus on this one moment. He'd moved from one human body to another, life after life, and pursued his goal of world domination by the *Tupay*.

Publius settled into the chair. Victor's call had come to him during his dream state last night. Now, while his latest physical body, that of Christian Campbell, was resting comfortably in a chair at his home in Edinburgh, Scotland, his astral body was at the headquarters for the *Tupay* army. He studied the Dark Lord. The man's face was lean, his eyes yellow like a wolf's, his nose aquiline. He was wearing a full beard, neatly trimmed. Publius knew the Dark Lord could assume any visage he wanted simply by desiring it.

"There is a team leaving the Vesica Piscis Foundation today," Victor told him without preamble. "While we can't get into the condo where Calen Hernandez and Reno Manchahi live and plan strategy for finding the emerald spheres, we can get to the airlines." Victor smiled as he looked across the desk at his protégé. Publius Hadrian had lived during the glory of ancient Rome. Hadrian's Wall in England had been named after him. The emperor of

Rome from 117 to 138 A.D., he had the foresight to order it built. As Publius lay dying, Victor had offered him immortality if he would join the *Tupay* army. That had appealed to Hadrian, and he'd taken the oath. From that point on, Victor had trained him and many other knights to become his personal military commanders on the field of battle against the Warriors for the Light.

"And where is this team going?" Publius asked.

"To your corner of the world—Great Britain. We have scanned the airline data and found their names on a passenger list, flying to London. From there, Drs. Kendra Johnson and Nolan Galloway will be renting a car. They have reservations to stay at Chalice Well in Glastonbury. What they do from that point on will be your business and your responsibility. They are going after the third sphere. We haven't been able to steal the other two, which are being kept at the Village of the Clouds, a fortress no *Tupay* can access. We need to get this third one, Publius."

"Your orders will be carried out, my lord," he said, nodding. "There is a woman who owns a bookshop in Glastonbury—Daria Whitcomb. She's not a knight, but she is *Tupay* and will assist us. She disguises herself as a Druidic priestess, and those who follow that religion have no idea who she really is." Publius smiled briefly. "I'd like to enlist her aid in following this *Taqe* team."

"That is fine with me, Publius." Victor examined

the warrior before him. Publius had moved into the body of Christian Campbell ten years earlier, when the Scot was twenty-five. For the most part, "Christian" liked his name and situation, wanted to stay in Great Britain, a favorite country of his through the last two thousand years of immortality. His face was square, his chin strong, and his cheeks ruddy. His mane of gold hair was neatly styled and fell across his broad shoulders. Victor was pleased that Publius had chosen the strong and robust body of a very rich man.

"Christian Campbell is a software millionaire many times over, so money shouldn't be a problem here," Victor said to the knight.

"Money to burn, as they say." Publius grinned at his lord. "I will contact Daria when I return to Edinburgh. And I'll also order one of my soldiers to tail them from a distance." Publius frowned. "Unfortunately, we can't get anywhere near Chalice Well."

"Why?"

"Because it's a *Taqe* stronghold, energywise, protected by the Village of the Clouds. The garden there holds a sacred spring that has never run dry. Its red water, stained with iron oxide, is believed to symbolize the blood of the Great Mother Goddess. A white spring nearby, influenced with calcium, symbolizes her male consort." Opening his large, square hands, Publius added, "All we can do is wait and watch. There's no way to move into the invisible realms to access the team, or hear their conversations. If any

Tupay tries to enter that place, it will raise an alarm. We want this team to think no one is watching or following them."

Rubbing his beard, Victor nodded. "This will become a cat-and-mouse game, then. We can only hope they'll go somewhere unprotected."

"My lord, while there are clearly places under the direct protection of *Taqe* energy, many are not. I'll have Daria follow their movements and report back to me. I want to remain in the background until I see an opening to win the team's trust. Then I'll get involved." He gave the Dark Lord a lethal smile.

"Excellent plan, Publius. Stay in touch with me. If necessary, I'll possess a human to help you get that sphere."

"Of course, my lord." Publius knew that a *Tupay* in spirit could possess anything in the third dimension. He could not, because he was already in body. But he had other skills he could use.

Publius rose and gave the traditional salute, clapping a clenched fist against his heart. "I live to do your bidding. May the *Tupay* energy continue to bless you."

"Thank you, Sir Hadrian. I take your words to heart." Lifting his hand, Victor said, "Now leave me."

He watched as Hadrian dissolved into the ether. The next second, Victor was alone. Outside his office, a veritable city of warriors moved and worked within the dark gray walls of the large castle. They lived in the Other Worlds, just as the *Taqe* stronghold, Village of the Clouds, did. Interdimensional warfare was nothing new to Victor.

Sighing, he closed his eyes and willed himself to Aguas Calientes, Peru, the jungle city where he'd last lived in human form. In an instant, Victor found himself hovering in a corner of the living room of his fine home. His heart wrenched when he saw his beloved wife, Fidelia, cradling his baby daughter, Abegail. She was breast-feeding. Grief momentarily struck Victor. When Mason Ridfort had killed his human body, Fidelia was left with no one to support her. Victor had quickly changed that by having another knight of the *Tupay* realm send her enough money to leave her well-off for the rest of her natural life. And to give his children a fine education.

Fidelia was *Tupay,* but she was mortal. Victor had never revealed to her who he really was. He had fallen in love with the Peruvian beauty, who came from the poor section of the town that sat at the foot of Machu Picchu. And she had loved him with such innocence and devotion that Victor truly pined for his wife, as he had few others in his four thousand years of life.

Baby Abegail suckled hungrily at her mother's small, rounded breast. Bubbles of milk played at each corner of her bow shaped mouth. Victor saw his wife smile tenderly down at their daughter. She began to sing a Quero lullaby, and it filled Victor with yearning. Perhaps he should possess another body and come back to her....

But the shock of a different man coming into her life and claiming to be her husband would not play out well, Victor knew. Fidelia held the superstitions of the Quero people, and would never accept him as the father of her children, her own husband if he were in another man's body. It would be too much for the simple woman.

Rage and hatred flowed through Victor as he thought of Mason Ridfort, who had slashed his throat during a fight at the base of Huaynu Picchu. Victor had been stalking his daughter, Ana, when Ridfort had appeared out of the jungle. Victor had hoped to seize the second emerald sphere, which his daughter had just found. His plans were dashed when Ridfort picked up his unveiled energy trail and, in jaguar form, slashed his throat open, nearly decapitating him. The body Victor had inhabited died that day, but he'd escaped into the Other Worlds in spirit form.

Damn Ridfort for taking him from that life, his family. Of all the women Victor had loved, Fidelia was his favorite.

Maybe he was being worn down by the stress and pressure of maintaining his kingship of the *Tupay*. And for now, he was ruling alone. Victor needed the family that Fidelia had lovingly provided him. She had carried his son, Marcial, ten years earlier. Victor had plans to make his son and his two-month-old daughter, Abegail, sole inheritors of his kingdom. When Marcial reached the age of fourteen, Victor would make him immortal, and then train him. When Abegail reached that age, he'd do the same with her. And then he'd have family who would rule with him. Victor would step down after the *Tupay* won the right to rule Earth.

Having lived these last four thousand years, he found that emotional ties he made and then lost wore him down. Kekuni, the last *Tupay* king, the one who had made Victor immortal, had confessed to the same fatigue. When given an opportunity to become like him, most of his wives and children saw it as a curse, not an opportunity. The old sorcerer had tiredly told Victor that one day he would be in that position himself. Victor had scoffed at him. But now, he understood. His master had lived four thousand years before releasing his immortality by a simple free choice.

Victor wondered if he himself would be killed off permanently. He had not anticipated the recent death of his human form by a *Taqe* warrior, but he'd made the mistake of focusing too much on his long-lost daughter, Ana. And he'd paid a heavy price for his distraction. Any *Tupay* could lose their immortality if they died with the body they inhabited. If they escaped the body before it died, they continued their immortality.

As he hovered in the corner of the room where

his wife rocked Abegail in her arms, Victor saw Marcial enter.

"Mama, can I go out and play? The rain has stopped. My friends want to skateboard down the hill. May I?"

Fidelia smiled softly at her ten-year-old son. "Just for an hour, Marcial. And then the tutor comes, and you must learn your mathematics."

Pouting, Marcial leaned his head against his mother's slender shoulder. "Oh, Mama…"

"You miss him so much, my son," Fidelia murmured, and placed a kiss on Marcial's tousled hair. "Your papa…you used to spend so much time with him. He was teaching you math, and then he would take you out for hikes and walks. You would help him in our store by putting on price tags and opening boxes." Sighing, Fidelia gazed at the boy. "Your papa still loves you. He always will. I feel he's here, visiting us today." She smiled tenderly at Marcial. "Do you feel him?"

He nodded. "I do, Mama." He rubbed his tear-filled eyes. "I miss Papa so much. I wish he would come back. What happened to him? Why did he leave us?"

"Oh, sweet boy," Fidelia said brokenly, "a jaguar killed him. We don't know why. Papa was just unlucky. But we will always keep the spirit of your father alive between us. Always."

Victor had to leave. He willed himself out of the

house and back to the Dark Castle. Sitting there once more, he rubbed his face with his hand. Tears fell from his eyes as he felt the wrenching pain and loss of his beloved son and daughter. There were times when he hated life. Over his many lifetimes, Victor had seen a number of *Tupay* decide to stop the process and die in the body they inhabited. If they died of natural causes, they would lose their immortality and move on into the flow of the Great Mother Goddess's plan for all souls. And if that occurred, they lost their *Tupay* status, as well. To Victor, that was unacceptable.

The *Tupay* way was the glorification of living a dual life, in any form. One could experience lust, greed, passion, jealousy, anger, joy and every other emotion not possible in spirit. The heavy energy of lesser emotions were stripped off as a person died and left an incarnation. But there was a group of souls who wanted these experiences time after time. They did not want to give them up to go to the Light.

The *Taqe* were just the opposite; they aspired to the higher, lighter vibration of selflessness, compassion and peace. Victor considered them the greatest enemy to his own chosen sybaritic way of life.

Turning to a book that showed the assembled Emerald Key necklace, Victor stared down at the illustration. The cosmic library in the Dark Castle held information on all secrets, myths and legends generated throughout the universe. Victor's focus was on

Earth, and he'd tirelessly studied all objects of power that had been created by man. He had strived to collect as many ceremonial items as he could for the *Tupay.* The most elusive had been the Emerald Key necklace, but now it was within his grasp, quite literally. Only it seemed the Great Mother Goddess was playing favorites and allowing the *Taqe,* Warriors for the Light, to find the spheres first.

Victor shrugged. He knew that possessing light energy was the focus of many souls. It took thousands of lifetimes of struggle for many humans to rise to the vaunted levels they aspired to. Not him. And not his kind. The *Tupay* looked for planets throughout the universe that gloried fully in the experience of living in the third dimension. There was nothing like the physical feeling of moving lustfully with a woman in heat. Victor savored sexual contact like the addict he had become. Sex was what he missed most while in spirit. No longer could he have hot intimacy with Fidelia, who was so earthy, passionate and willing. She had been a consummate lover and had come unstrung beneath his searching hands, mouth and teeth. As innocent as she seemed, she was a whore inside, and he'd held heaven in his arms when he was with her.

But no more. Not since Ridfort had taken his human form away from him. Victor wanted to get even with the *Taqe* warrior. There was nothing he wanted more than to kill him, but that had to wait.

Right now he had to focus on seizing this third emerald before the team from the foundation took it back to Quito with them. If that was accomplished, they would rush it off to the Village of the Clouds, where it would stay.

Being in spirit form allowed Victor access to all dimensions. He heard the noise and laughter outside his massive office. There were *Tupay* being trained and educated here nonstop. They did not lack for volunteers from Earth who wanted to pursue their way of life. If anything, power was the greatest lure to the candidates who came here during their sleep state, or who traveled astrally for training. Yes, the aphrodisiac all *Tupays* lusted after was power. With it, they could control the life they wanted.

Smiling, Victor settled back into his black leather chair. He closed his eyes and clasped his hands in his lap, veiling himself so that his aura and energy signature could not be picked up by the *Taqe* team.

Victor did not know these people who were after the sphere. Hadrian would immediately investigate their identities and backgrounds. But despite the help from his warriors, Victor found his curiosity getting the better of him, and he decided to check out the couple on their flight to England. What would he find? Would they be anything like Mace Ridfort, or his lost daughter, Ana?

To Victor's deep regret, Ana had chosen the Light.

Worse, she and Ridfort had married, combining their
energies that created a nasty simmering rage within
Victor. His own daughter, a child from his loins, had
become a traitor to the *Tupay* way of life! He still
wrestled with those emotions because Ana had been
the woman of the legends, intended to be his consort
in ruling Earth.

And with her refusal, Victor had lost the first
major battle in this war. He wasn't going to lose the
next round. Taking a deep breath, he cloaked himself
and went into the airliner.

It was easy to spot Warriors for the Light. Their
auras always consisted of rainbow colors. Most
people's auras were washed out in comparison. A
Taqe's was bright, scintillating, intensely colorful—
impossible to miss.

As Victor moved into the first-class section and
hid in the galley, he spotted the two immediately.
They sat in the first row on the left. Raising his
brows, he noticed a lot of red and black in their auras.
Hmm, that was interesting. Red meant anger and
black meant grief or depression. Usually *Taqe* auras
were clear and clean, but these two seemed dirty.

Victor smiled as he watched them. The woman
had red hair and flashing green eyes. Very pretty. Her
partner was powerful, so Victor was glad he'd veiled
himself. Something about the man's startling blue
eyes put him on guard. This guy was a hunter, just
as Mason Ridfort was. Hunters among the Warriors

for the Light had special skills that could fatally harm any *Tupay*. Wary, Victor focused his hearing to eavesdrop on their conversation.

"I told you, Nolan, I don't like the fact we have to work together. I'm doing this for Harvard."

"Glad you've got your priorities straight," Nolan murmured. "Never mind peace in the world. Go, Harvard." He lifted his fist to underscore his drily spoken words.

Glaring at him, Kendra whispered in fury, "Go to hell, Nolan! You haven't a clue what humane behavior is!"

"I think I do."

Kendra crossed her legs, turning away from him. She was glad the seats were wide, with plenty of space between them. No way did she want any physical contact with Nolan Galloway! She didn't like his smirk or the glittering, dangerous look in his narrowed eyes. "Your overconfidence got my sister killed. So don't talk to me about humane or compassionate behavior. If you'd been less cocky and less of a know-it-all, she'd be alive today."

Scowling, Nolan felt the back of his neck prickle, which was always a sign of danger. He scanned the cabin, but saw nothing out of place. Yet this reaction had saved his life many times in the past. So what was happening now that was dangerous? Oh, Kendra was clearly angry at him, but she didn't have it in her to kill him. Rubbing his neck, the site of his

Vesica Piscis birthmark, Nolan couldn't figure out where the feeling of foreboding came from.

"Do you feel anything?" he asked Kendra, who shot a glare in his direction. "No, I'm serious," he said. "I feel danger. Nearby."

"All I feel is *you*. And I'm mad as hell at you, Nolan. If I could, I'd get out of this seat and go sit somewhere else, but this flight is completely full." Her nostrils flared. "You're the danger."

Unable to shake the feeling, Nolan let her words bounce off him like water off a duck's back. His attention was drawn to the station where the flight attendants were preparing lunch. Something was in there. But what? He wanted to point his finger toward the area, to see what moved or changed, but he didn't dare, under the circumstances. And then, as soon as he had the thought, the sense of danger disappeared.

Stymied, Nolan continued to stare into the galley, where two flight attendants were working with trays of food. What had just happened?

Sighing, he switched his attention back to Kendra. They'd fought all across the Atlantic. In three hours, they would land in London. Would her fury abate by then? Could they stop the angry exchanges long enough to rent a car and drive to Glastonbury? Maybe being at Chalice Well, a protected *Taqe* garden, would soothe Kendra's hatred of him.

Nolan could only hope.

Chapter 4

As they picked up their rental car after landing at Heathrow, Nolan felt danger again. The sky was a desultory gray, with light rain, typical for England at this time of year, he supposed. The car, a silver Toyota hybrid Corolla, was waiting for them. Tossing the luggage into the trunk, Nolan looked around as Kendra got in on the right-hand side, preparing to drive.

The lot was busy with airline passengers picking up rental cars. His neck prickled with the same feeling he'd had on the plane. As his gaze swung from right to left, he spotted a man standing two rows away, watching them, his hands in the pockets of his black raincoat. He was middle-aged, with a dark brown beard, and was wearing a black hat. As soon as his gaze met Nolan's, the stranger turned away and busied himself with his rental car.

Okay, maybe he was overdramatizing Reno and Calen's warning about the *Tupay*, Nolan decided. He walked to the passenger side of the vehicle and slid in. The warning that Guerra could possess their bodies and kill them when exiting again bothered him. As he glanced over at Kendra, who was pointedly ignoring him, he worried about her. Why wasn't she taking their mission more seriously? Nolan supposed he knew the answer to that question. She was wrapped up in the past, her rage bubbling up between them like hot lava, scorching his soul. She wasn't focused on the present at all.

"Are you ready?" Kendra demanded. She turned the key, and the engine purred to life. She got the windshield wipers working. Rain depressed her, and she was feeling a lot of weight on her shoulders right now. She knew she had to stop taking chunks out of Galloway, but how? Just being with him sent her emotions seesawing from rage to desire. It disturbed her that after nearly a decade, she would still be drawn to him. Her hands gripped the wheel until her knuckles whitened.

"Yeah, I'm ready," he muttered, quickly fastening the seat belt across his body. "I'll give you directions on how to escape this mess of an airport so we can be on our way to Glastonbury."

"Good. Heathrow is always a nightmare to get out of," she said, putting the car in Drive.

As they sped out of the rain-slick lot, Nolan made a point of checking out the stranger in the black raincoat two rows over. He was in a black BMW and didn't lift his head to look at them. Maybe Nolan had imagined the danger, but he'd stayed alert.

Rubbing his neck, he glanced at Kendra. Her profile was elegant, and reminded him of a bust of Nefertiti that had been dug up by archaeologists over a century ago. Kendra was as beautiful as the Egyptian queen.

Unfortunately, there was no way for Nolan to make peace within his heart. He wanted Kendra all over again. And in every conceivable way.

Stymied and frustrated, he tried to concentrate on the map and keep an eye out for the *Tupay*. In his gut, he sensed them nearby. Like hounds from hell on their heels, he supposed. And above all, Nolan needed to protect Kendra, who still seemed completely oblivious to the danger.

"How far to Glastonbury?" she asked. "I've been to England many times, on digs up north, but I've never been to the southwestern portion."

Looking ahead at the heavy traffic crawling around the huge airport, Nolan said, "When we finally get out of this bloody construction, we take a main freeway, and Glastonbury is about three hours away. But this rain and these drivers could add another hour."

Kendra glanced at Nolan. His brow was bunched, his hair damp from the rain and tousled. He didn't wear a hat, preferring to feel the sun and the wind. "You haven't lost your unique brand of humor, I see." When Kendra saw Nolan lift his head, his incredible blue eyes meeting and holding hers for that moment, she felt heat flush through her and her lower body stir to life. He was so damn sensual. Those eyes of his were always her undoing. A woman could drown, die and be reborn in them. And Kendra recalled too easily the times they'd made love like wild animals, their passion flaring and Nolan's eyes burning with desire for her. Gulping, she tore her gaze from his and concentrated on the nasty traffic, which was four lanes wide and moving at three or four miles per hour.

Nolan suggested they get into the left lane. "You gotta admit, Heathrow traffic is constipation at its finest."

"For once we agree on something," Kendra muttered as she forced her way left.

"Hey, it's a start," Nolan laughed, relief tunneling through him as he saw her mouth finally curve in a genuine smile. Hope flared within him. How badly he wanted Kendra to forgive him for what had happened. Forgive. Yes, he needed that from her. It was a bittersweet knife in his heart.

"I'd sure like to give Heathrow officials an enema," Kendra said, her grin broadening as she maneuvered through backed-up traffic.

Giving an evil chuckle, Nolan pointed to a sign and told her to take the next left turn. "Where's the enema bag? I'll do it personally."

Her mood lightened because of Nolan's infectious humor. She saw the laugh lines deepen around the corners of his eyes. When he flashed that cockeyed Irish smile, dimples appeared and made him look boyishly appealing. A decade might have lapsed, but Nolan was still the same rogue she'd fallen in love with.

"Ahh," he said as they finally reached the motorway on-ramp. "We're free at last…"

Nodding, Kendra sped onto the freeway. There were plenty of cars at 8:00 a.m., all business traffic, but at least they were moving at a brisk pace compared to the snarl around Heathrow. "Have you ever been to Glastonbury?"

Nolan nodded and switched maps. "Yeah, once. A long time ago. There was an archaeology lecture on the Tor, that manmade hill that looms above the town. I was there for a week, touring."

"So you know the lay of the land around there," Kendra said. As she flicked a glance in the rearview mirror, she noticed a black BMW following her. It had stayed on her tail since the airport. Maybe she was being jumpy, she thought, deciding not to share her observation with Nolan. If the vehicle followed them into Glastonbury, she'd let him know.

"I got to go over Avebury, the Neolithic stone

circle about an hour away. There's another tor. The Salisbury Plain where all these neolithic monuments and burial chambers are located is full of archaeological treasures."

"Where's Windmill Hill in comparison to all of this stuff?" Kendra asked. The rain was lightening considerably as they sped along the freeway, and the traffic had dissolved to a trickle.

"It's northwest of Glastonbury, in Wiltshire. It's located close to the Avebury stone circle, and I believe there's an energetic connection between them." Nolan looked around at the lush agricultural lands on both sides of the motorway. It reminded him of a colorful quilt of blues, greens and yellows. "And the majority of crop circles appear in that same area," Nolan informed her. He was glad they were talking like reasonable human beings now. The sniping and anger on the plane had left him feeling ragged and out of sorts.

"Why do you think that is?"

Shrugging, Nolan said, "The Druid culture was here long before Christianity. It was an earth-centered religion. The Druids knew Mother Earth is alive, and they communicated with her. Most people associate them with oak groves, but they worked with nature in her many forms." Nolan gestured to the landscape around them. "The Druids were aware of the ley lines—flows of energy—that crisscross the country. Where the energy lines intersect, they built stone circles, or planted rings of trees such as at Woodhenge, which is near Stonehenge. They often held ceremonies there. And they built barrows, and placed tumuli, where they buried people. There are dolmans or standing stones in certain key areas that help keep the energy moving. You'll see all these things in southwest England. It's a hotbed of ley line activity, and the Neolithic people knew it before the Druids ever came on the scene."

"So people have worked with Mother Earth and her energy lines since the Stone Age?"

"Precisely," Nolan said, pleased that she seemed interested in the amazing cultures he'd studied in depth over the years. "I didn't know you knew so much about them. Your expertise is more in South American and Middle Eastern sites."

"I've changed my focus over the years, Nolan." There, she'd said his name without feeling angry. For the first time in a decade. Somehow, just the sound of it sent a thrumming sensation through Kendra's heart. The rage she'd felt toward him was dissolving. She felt she should be civil to him for the duration of this mission. And she could see that Nolan was trying his best to get along with her. "I've been working on an article regarding Iron Age forts here in southwestern England."

"Why am I not surprised? I like the synchronicity. I'm sure whatever I'm telling you, you already know, and then some."

Nolan had always respected her knowledge, and Kendra glowed inwardly when he gave her an admiring look. Tearing her gaze from his, she paid attention to her driving.

"In your studies, Kendra, did crop circles come up?" he asked.

"They have," Kendra said, relieved to be talking with Nolan on an academic level. It was a safe place to be with him. "Crop circles are not just a modern thing, Nolan. I believe you know that."

"Yes. Throughout history, these mysterious patterns have appeared around the world. I've seen cave paintings of them in France. And in aboriginal art in Australia. Crop circles are an ancient phenomena, there is no question."

"What do you think makes them? I know there's a battle raging between 'croppies'—the circles are Mother Earth talking to humanity—and hard-headed science types who say they are fraudulent and manmade."

"And therefore unimportant," Nolan finished. He rubbed his stubbled chin. "Some modern crop circles *have* been created by people, but I've seen others that I don't believe were. And how do you account for all the evidence of crop circles in other times and cultures? Were they made by humans or by gods or goddesses that individuals of that culture believed in? It's a dilemma, for sure."

"And yet we're supposed to sit out on Windmill

Hill and wait for one to appear." Kendra shook her head and turned off the windshield wipers. "Does that mean we'll be catching a couple of guys with two-by-fours smashing down fields of wheat?"

"Or does it mean we'll see something fantastic happen?" Nolan traded a smile with her.

"You really believe Calen's vision will come true? That those specific symbols she drew will really appear in a farm field?"

"That's why we're here, isn't it?" Nolan rubbed his hands together with glee. "I don't know about you, but I'm looking forward to putting up a tent, throwing down a sleeping bag and using my night-vision binoculars to scan the fields throughout the night. I feel something *will* happen."

Kendra snorted softly. "Yeah, we'll sneak up on the guys crushing the wheat."

"Be a good scientist," Nolan chided good-humoredly. "Stay open-minded. Don't draw a con-clusion until you see the evidence."

The gentle warmth between them made Kendra relax at last. As they drove southward, they had only truck traffic to contend with. "Okay, okay, you're right. But until I see it with my own two eyes, I'm going to believe it's human beings defrauding us with these strange circles and patterns."

Grinning, Nolan said, "Well, we'll both be there to see, won't we? But first things first. We've got to get to Glastonbury and over to the Chalice Well. The

Michael House is rented out for us, so we'll be able to check in and leave most of our stuff there. We'll keep the camping equipment in the car and head back to Wiltshire county right after that."

"Busy day," Kendra agreed. And she was glad. She didn't want idle time with Nolan. He was too easy on the eyes and too hard on her heart. Nolan had aged gracefully and seemed to be more mature than before. All of that appealed to Kendra, and as she drove, she was all too aware of his proximity. He was too close. Getting to Chalice Well would give her the space she desperately needed from his Irish banter, his boyish smile and those penetrating blue eyes of his.

"Oh, this is beautiful," Kendra murmured as she stood at the wrought-iron gate to Chalice Well. She instantly recognized the Vesica Piscis symbol of two overlapping rings welded into the gate. Nolan was at the office window, discussing their reservation with a gray-haired woman there.

The gate had a trellis, with pink roses climbing overtop and their fragrance filled the air. The wide steps were of ochre and gray stone. Kendra saw that the double ring motif had been placed in the path, as well. She felt the energy of the garden, refreshingly vital and peaceful after the plane ride and the drive from Heathrow. The sun was peeking between the ragged, scudding clouds, drying up the humidity.

Nolan turned, holding up the key to the Michael House, situated across the road from Chalice Well. "Let's go."

Kendra wanted to take time to go explore the garden, but resisted. It was noon and her stomach was growling with hunger. As she followed Nolan back down the rock path, she said, "How about going to a pub in Glastonbury as soon as we get done putting our luggage in the house?"

"Sounds good to me," he said, admiring the multicolored daisies and pansies blooming on both sides of the stone path. "I'm starved."

Kendra shook her head. "Nothing has changed with you, has it? You had a hollow leg when I knew you before." Nolan had eaten like a proverbial draft horse when Kendra had lived with him, and yet he was as lean as a wolf. "If I ate like you did, I'd be three hundred pounds by now, Galloway."

Nolan twisted to look at her, and laughed. "Well, *some* things have changed, Kendra. But my food intake? No, it's the same. I eat anything that doesn't move first." He continued to chuckle as they reached the car in the small parking lot below Chalice Well.

After unlocking the Toyota, Kendra smiled and climbed in. "You'd chase it down and catch it if you had to. Nothing is safe from you."

Nolan laughed again. "Have lunch with me at the English Kitchen in town and see just how much I can eat."

She shook her head and backed the car out. As she did, she saw a black BMW slowly cruising along the thoroughfare between Chalice Well and the Michael House. Frowning, she asked, "Do you see that black car, Nolan?"

"Yeah. Why?"

Kendra waited for traffic to clear and then drove across the highway to the Michael House parking lot. "I saw one like that when we got this rental car at Heathrow. It followed us onto the freeway. Do you think it might be the same one? And that the driver is a *Tupay?*"

Nolan watched the car disappear around the curve. "I don't know. It's too much of a coincidence to think it might be just a tourist. He probably is a tail." Maybe that was why Nolan's neck had prickled back there. "I picked up on him, too. I saw a guy in a black raincoat staring at us in the rental area. Did you see him?"

"No, I didn't. I guess I wasn't paying attention like I should have," Kendra said, shutting off the engine and climbing out. Michael House was a century-old, two-story stone structure. She liked the Victorian feel to it, from the gabled slate roof to the multicolored stone façade.

"Well," Nolan said, opening the trunk of the car and taking out their luggage, "let's keep our eyes peeled. If the dude shows up at the English Kitchen, we'll know for sure he was tailing us. A black BMW is going to stick out in the parking lot."

Kendra hefted a couple of pieces of luggage and they trooped to the entrance. "And then what? What do we do? Pull out our lightsabers and do battle with the guy?"

Nolan opened the door and stood aside so Kendra could haul in her luggage. Then he followed her through the large living room and up the carpeted stairs to the two bedrooms on the second floor. "We're not exactly *Star Wars* types," he said half-jokingly.

"Then how do we defend ourselves?"

"Calen said love your enemy. I guess that's all we've got going for us."

Grimacing, Kendra halted at the first door, painted emerald green. "Right. The guy is aiming a pistol in my face and I'm supposed to send him love. Helluva trade-off, if you ask me."

Raising his brows, Nolan eased past her. "Right now, that's our only option."

"Have you ever tried it?"

"No, no one has held a gun in my face, so I didn't have to." He grinned.

Kendra reluctantly returned his smile. "You're not much help, Galloway! See you in a few minutes downstairs."

She opened the door and stepped inside what turned out to be a beautifully decorated bedroom. White curtains draped the window; a brown-and-gold spread covered the queen-size bed. There was an antique cherry dresser, and an old-fashioned hand-painted glass lamps on each bedstand. A vase of red, purple and yellow tulips sat on the dresser, and she liked the soft, sunny yellow wallpaper.

As she dropped her luggage on the floor, Kendra heard Nolan clumping down the hall to his room. She immediately headed to her ensuite bathroom, eager to freshen up. Though she was dead on her feet, having lunch was her first priority, and it wasn't long before she was hurrying back down the stairs. Nolan was standing in the living room, waiting for her.

"Let me buy you lunch," he said.

Kendra knew they had an expense account with the V. P. Foundation, which would in any case be picking up the tab. If Nolan were going to buy her a meal from his own pocket, she'd have said no. They could each pay their way.

She couldn't let down her guard with him, she realized. If she did, her silly heart would reach out to him, just as it had so many years earlier.

Shaking her head, she followed him back out to the car. She wasn't about to fall for him again. Not a chance in hell.

Chapter 5

"This was my favorite hangout when I was last here," Nolan confided to Kendra as they sat down at a dark wooden table in a corner of the pub. "Good grub," he assured her. The noon crowd had filled the eatery, and Nolan wasn't at all surprised by its ongoing popularity. He shook out his white linen napkin and laid it across his lap. Best of all, it was smoke-free.

"Nice vibes in here," Kendra noted as she opened her menu. The restaurant bustled with activity, but it wasn't noisy. No earsplitting music blared to ruin the ambience. A good thing, for Kendra had such sensitive ears she couldn't stay in loud restaurants. Of course, the quiet atmosphere made it impossible to ignore Nolan's presence. And when she peeked over the menu at him, he was watching her. Instantly, her breasts tightened in response to his burning look. She couldn't help but be shocked over the discovery that Nolan still wanted her. How could he, after all that had happened?

"I'd suggest the lamb," he told her, quickly dousing the hunger he felt toward Kendra. Damn, she looked desirable in her casual clothes. No matter what she wore, Nolan wanted her. The pale pink tee beneath her ivory canvas vest only accented her skin tones and showed off her fine collarbone. Her red hair was streaked with blond and burgundy highlights. The strands were thick and curled sensuously about her proud shoulders. But it was those green eyes dappled with gold that always drew Nolan. When he saw her eyes widen with surprise, he glanced back at his menu. Kendra has sensed intuitively that he was gazing at her. She had always been psychic, but now, it seemed, was even more so. He'd have to be careful not to look at her like a lovesick puppy.

"The lamb?" Kendra scowled and scanned the offerings on the menu. Anything to break the sudden tension that had sprung between them. "That looks fine."

The waitress came over and Nolan ordered for them. When she hurried away, he was about to speak, but then a shadow fell across him. Instantly, the back of his neck started burning, a warning of high danger. Snapping his head to the left, Nolan saw a large, ruddy-faced man approaching.

"Dr. Kendra Johnson?" the stranger rumbled in a Scottish burr, thrusting out his hand toward her. "What a pleasant surprise. Perhaps you remember me from your presentation in London? At the British Museum last year, about women's roles during the Iron Age in England? Allow me to introduce myself. I'm Christian Campbell, from Edinburgh."

Kendra heard the low, well-modulated growl of a male voice, then eyed the tall, beefy Scot standing before her. Blinking, she stared at the rough square hand being held out toward her. "Uh, I'm sorry, Mr. Campbell, I don't recall meeting you, but thank you for remembering my talk."

Kendra slid her hand into his. His catlike, golden-brown eyes sparkled with such vitality and life. Surely she'd remember this man.

But then her head spun, and she felt suddenly dizzy for some reason.

"Well, there was a crowd of over two hundred people at your lecture," Christian replied with a chuckle. He released her hand. "So I'm not surprised you don't recall. I'm just an amateur archaeologist, and you were surrounded by the cream of the European archaeology community."

Kendra found it difficult to think. Her hand burned briefly where Christian Campbell had touched it. Quickly pulling it back, she stammered, "This—this is my colleague, Professor Nolan Galloway of Princeton."

The instant Nolan shook the large Scot's hand, he felt an icy warning of danger. The man was dressed like a professional, in a suit and tie. Only Campbell's thick mane of sun-streaked blond hair took away from the neat look, instead hinting at an untamed wildness.

"Nice to meet you, Mr. Campbell," Nolan said. Why the hell was he feeling like a three-alarm fire was about to break out? Clearly, Campbell only had eyes for Kendra. And jealousy ate through Nolan when he saw the Scot wasn't wearing a wedding band. He had an expensive-looking dark leather bag hung casually over his broad shoulder, and wore a Rolex watch. This man was rich, no doubt.

Kendra felt flustered, and her hand was burning. When she'd connected with Campbell's rough flesh, sudden pictures of a proud, arrogant Roman emperor standing on a rock wall had flashed before her. And then she'd felt grief, longing, and a sense of a hunter stalking his prey. Just as quickly as those images came, they were gone. Her psychometry gift meant that if she shook hands with anyone, Kendra would receive information, whether she wanted it or not. As she stared up at the massive and powerful man, she could see he had certain Roman features. Military in bearing, Christian Campbell reminded her of a wolf in sheep's clothing. And the back of her neck, where her birthmark lay, was burning like fire.

Rubbing it without thinking, Kendra said, "Mr. Campbell, would you like to join us for lunch? We just ordered."

Nolan scowled. "Dr. Johnson, I'm sorry, but we're here to discuss business." He gave Campbell a cool look and a silent warning. "Perhaps another time, Mr. Campbell?"

Christian smiled warmly. "Of course, Professor. Are you here on a dig, may I ask?"

Not liking the feeling of energy crawling around outside his aura, Nolan bristled inwardly. As he glanced across the table at Kendra, he noticed that she seemed confused by the Scot. Campbell's wide, intelligent eyes were trained on her like a hawk hunting his next meal. Nolan yanked his focus back to the stranger. "I'm afraid we can't divulge much other than we're here on business, Mr. Campbell."

"Ah, I see. Well, I just wanted to come over and introduce myself." He gave Kendra a dazzling smile. "The last time you were here, Dr. Johnson, you were single and unattached. May I presume that is still so?"

Raising her eyebrows at his bold inquiry, Kendra said, "Uh, yes. I don't have any serious relationship right now, Mr. Campbell." The man was positively handsome, though blatantly forward. Kendra's womanly instincts were on alert. She tried to reconnect with the image of the Roman emperor, clad in golden armor, with a purple cape around his broad shoulders. When she gazed into Christian's gleaming brown eyes, however, she saw a Scotsman, not a Roman.

"Ah, good news indeed. May I inquire as to where you're staying, Doctor?"

"The Michael House," Kendra said.

Christian nodded and took a step back. "Excellent. Doctor, I do hope you're staying here a few days?"

"Yes, we are."

Rubbing his hands together, the man beamed. "You'll be hearing from me. In the meantime, enjoy your business luncheon." He smiled warmly and walked back to his small table across the room.

Nolan scowled as he watched the man retreat, then turned his focus back on Kendra. "You all right? You look pale."

Waving her hand, she said, "I don't remember him, Nolan. But there were over two hundred people at my lecture in London last year."

"He's not an easy man to forget," Nolan drawled. The waitress came with their order, setting steaming platters of lamb, mashed potatoes and green peas in front of them.

Kendra picked up her cutlery. "You're right. I'd remember him. For sure."

Nolan felt his heart clench. He understood what she meant. "What happened when he shook hands with you? Did you pick up on something?"

Slicing into the fragrant lamb, which had been braised and seasoned with rosemary, Kendra said, "Yes, I do." She took a bite, chewed and swallowed before she spoke. "It was so odd, Nolan. I saw a Roman—an emperor, I think, or some kind of leader. He was standing on this white limestone wall, his fist raised in the air in celebration. Soldiers surrounded him, and they were all shouting and happy."

"What was so odd about the image?"

Shrugging, Kendra nudged some peas into the dark brown gravy. "Somehow, it connects to Campbell. When I shake hands with a person, I see flashes of their life." She pointed to her brow. "It's like a movie screen in front of me. The scene overlays the present, and I see it, not them, for a moment. I also get a feeling around that scene—unless I'm really exhausted. Then, I don't get much of anything." Kendra popped some peas into her mouth and frowned in concentration. She was trying to feel her way through her experience with Campbell.

"So could this have been Campbell's past life?" Nolan pressed.

They were speaking avidly now, the type of conversation she often used to have with Nolan. At first, she wanted to resist it, but finding the emerald sphere and exchanging information was more important. "Well, if it was a past life of his, that's a first for me. I've never seen past lives before. Just a person's present life."

"I don't have your gift, but I picked up a three-alarm warning," Nolan muttered as he ate. Shooting Kendra a glance, he added, "Didn't you feel the danger?"

"Now that you mention it, the back of my neck felt like it was on fire." She rubbed the area again, which seemed to settle now that Campbell had left.

Nolan knew she possessed the same Vesica Piscis birthmark that he did. He'd discovered it the first day they'd met, at a multiuniversity dig. Her red hair had been gathered up in a ponytail, with the mark exposed. He'd often wondered if the magic of that symbol had drawn them together. Their first conversation had been about their mutual birthmark. Not that they fully knew back then what it meant. Calen and Reno had enlightened them about it. Nolan liked the idea that they were Warriors for the Light, on a mission of peace for the Earth. And that others with the same birthmark were on the mission with them.

"My birthmark smarts and burns when I'm in danger," Nolan confided in a low tone. "Does yours?"

"Mine, too. It felt like it was burning through my skin when Campbell shook hands with me. But he was friendly, Nolan. He certainly didn't pose any danger to us. I think he wanted to invite me out on a date." She smiled.

Nolan swallowed his jealousy. He could see that Kendra was interested in the amateur archaeologist. Just when Nolan was trying to patch things up between them, she became starry-eyed over a brazen Scot. There was no romantic relationship between them now, and Kendra was free to pursue her own private life. The idea hurt Nolan more than he could fathom, and his stomach clenched. "That's your privilege," he managed to reply in a strangled tone. "But we're here on business, Kendra. If that dude thinks he can just waltz over here and throw flowers and chocolate at you—"

"Whoa, Nolan." She held up her hands. "My private life is off-limits to you. You and I are going to find the sphere together—and that's all."

Stung, he pushed his food around on the plate with his fork. "You're right," he finally said, after the waitress had cleared the table. He poured his tea and noticed Kendra looking in the direction of Pretty Boy Campbell. What was she thinking? Hadn't she sensed danger when he'd come to their table? Dammit, anyway.

"You know," Nolan said, trying to be tactful, "Calen and Reno warned us about the *Tupay*. They travel in disguise. Campbell had his hair down over his neck, so we couldn't see if he carries the *Tupay* birthmark."

Shrugging, Kendra sipped her coffee. "He doesn't *feel* evil, Nolan. Maybe to you, but not to me. He was warm and engaging." She saw the resentment in Nolan's narrowed eyes as he held her gaze. "And he isn't wearing a wedding ring."

"So? He could be married, and took it off to meet you. He could be looking for a mistress." Nolan tried to keep the sarcasm from his voice.

"I think we should just focus on our assignment."

"Done." Nolan sat up and glanced across the restaurant. The Scot was gone. When had he left?

Relieved, Nolan said, "Listen, we need to return to the Michael House, sort out our gear and drive over to Windmill Hill." He glanced at his watch. The leather band had been scarred on many digs and the timepiece, a Bulova, was like an old friend to him. "It's 1:00 p.m. We should get set up, then check out the fields around the hill."

Setting her cup aside, Kendra nodded. "Let's do it."

The night was cool and damp as Kendra stood on the ramparts of the Neolithic fort atop Windmill Hill. The sun had set an hour earlier and the darkness was nearly complete. And the wind was picking up. As she pulled her yellow canvas jacket closer to her body, Kendra was thankful to have her Peruvian alpaca hat on.

Turning, she listened for Nolan's movements. The ramparts of the fort were huge mounds of earth, obviously the backbreaking work of many people in ages past. Abandoned long ago, they were covered by grass, which held the clay soil in place. Judging by the beam of Nolan's flashlight, he had just finished putting their sleeping bags into the nylon tent.

They had agreed that they'd take turns keeping watch, with one of them sleeping while the other scanned the four wheat fields that surrounded the hill.

Kendra glanced up and saw a few stars twinkling bravely above her. Stargazing in England was tough because, as an island in the Atlantic Ocean, it was often blanketed by fog. She enjoyed watching the stars, and savored the silence. In the distance, she could see a cluster of lights, likely the village near the Avebury stone circle. As she looked at the fields below, Kendra noticed a few lights from farmhouses. Wiltshire was an agricultural county, without much light pollution.

Nolan rejoined her, the night-vision binoculars swinging across his chest while he climbed the tallest rampart. "All quiet on the western front?" he asked, coming up beside her, but keeping his distance. Kendra stood with her hands tucked in the pockets of her bright yellow jacket. It was easy to spot her even in the dark.

"Seems to be." She couldn't see Nolan's face, just the vague, dark shape of his profile. Earlier, when they'd gone back to Michael House, Kendra had found a dozen red roses in a vase on the porch. They were from Christian Campbell, with an invitation to join him for lunch at the English Kitchen tomorrow at noon. He'd left his cell phone number. Nolan had been irritable ever since.

Why would he be jealous? she wondered. They had no personal relationship. And she was interested in the handsome Scot. There was something incredibly mesmerizing about him, and attractive. Nolan's warning that he might be *Tupay* was an overreaction. Besides, she could handle herself.

"I don't think any crop circle is going to magically appear," Kendra said. "I don't doubt Calen's vision, but this is pretty far-fetched." She waved her hand toward the dark fields below them.

Nolan raised his binoculars and scanned the area. "You forget one thing, Kendra," he said. "She and Reno already have two of the emerald spheres in their possession. And in each case, they were retrieved thanks to Calen's dreams." Lowering the field glasses, he studied her clean profile, backlit by the rising moon. "Don't dismiss Calen or her ability."

"You *really* think a crop circle will appear because we're here?" Kendra's voice dripped with skepticism.

"Yes, I believe it."

She chuckled. "That Irish side of you, the dreamer, is at it again, Galloway."

Nolan smiled and simply savored their closeness. At least she wasn't sniping at him. Maybe because her heart was set on that gold-maned Scot?

Nolan frowned. "I'll take my dreamer side anytime," he replied lightly. "I sort of like my mysticism."

Kendra gave a sharp laugh. "I suppose you still do your card tricks?"

"Of course," he murmured, pleased that she remembered. "I'm pretty good at them. I donate my time and talents to children's charities around the world. I'll often go to a local orphanage and put on a show for them."

At that moment, Kendra's heart twinged. She had accompanied him a number of times when he'd performed, and because Nolan was a child at heart, children everywhere fell in love with his big Irish smile and warm, open heart. Despite everything, Kendra found *herself* being drawn to him. To his gentle teasing, his smile, which always lifted her spirits, and those dancing blue eyes. Groaning internally, she tried to suppress all her memories and desires. Part of her wanted Nolan again. But it could never be. She couldn't deal with that.

"Hey!"

"What?"

"Look! Look over there to the east!"

Gasping, Kendra saw what appeared to be gold balls of light about ten feet above the ground. Instantly, she raised her video camera and fumbled for the switch. The glowing lights were dancing, as if alive, moving swiftly around the field. Several balls got together, hovered for a moment, and then raced away again. Heart pounding, Kendra tried to hold the camera steady as she filmed.

"Could it be people down there with flashlights?" she demanded breathlessly.

"Hell, no! They're moving too fast. My God, Kendra, this is *it!* This is what's making those crop circles! You're recording it, aren't you?"

"Yes, I am." She watched in excitement as the shimmering lights, hundreds of them now, darted around the field.

"I wonder if they're making that crop circle Calen saw in her dream?" Nolan stated, his binoculars trained on the shining balls of light. What were they? What was causing them? Giddiness thrummed through him, his pulse racing as he watched the event unfolding before them.

"I don't know," Kendra whispered, stunned. The lights seemed to be making a lot of curves and circles. She itched to run down the hill and into the field, but that would be difficult on such a dark night.

"They're gone!"

Blinking, Kendra realized the lights had suddenly disappeared. "Oh…" She swung the video camera around, in case they'd moved elsewhere.

But the night had returned to normal. The field was empty once more.

Nolan turned to peruse the other fields. They were dark, as well. No more balls of golden light. "What the hell did we just see, Kendra?"

"I wish I knew." She turned off the video recorder with shaky fingers, as Nolan completed a second scan of the fields with his binoculars.

"I guess we'll have to wait until dawn," he muttered unhappily. "Let's see if you caught anything on tape."

"I need to get the flashlight. I can't see the controls out here to rewind this thing. We'll go back to the tent."

"Right." Nolan started down the steep hill.

In the tent, Kendra sat cross-legged, with Nolan crouched next to her. They couldn't help touching because the screen on the video camera was small. She could feel his energy, breathed in his masculine scent, as he leaned over her shoulder to peer at the images. There was a comfort in having him close, she realized. She'd been scared to death when those lights appeared, and was glad for Nolan's quiet, steadying presence now. Kendra was still shaking from the experience.

"You got them!" Nolan crowed triumphantly. He pointed to the monitor. "Look at that! We've got crop circle makers on film! That's a helluva thing! You'll be famous for this."

"Just what I want—to be considered a crop circle expert. Galloway, I have a reputation to protect. I don't want to be called a croppie."

Laughing heartily, Nolan eased away from Kendra, but with reluctance. He loved the sweet, gingery scent of her shampoo, and enjoyed the warm closeness as they'd viewed the film. "Don't worry," he answered, patting her shoulder. "Your good name won't be ruined just by filming these lights."

The moment he touched Kendra's shoulder, he

felt an electric spark shoot up his hand and into his arm. It was a pleasant sensation, evoking many other, more intimate times. As he lifted his hand away, he realized he'd overstepped his bounds.

He moved to the other side of the tent as Kendra shut off the video and put it back into its leather case. "We have a choice here," he stated. "We can stay in this tent and freeze our butts off. Or we can drive an hour and stay at the Michael House in a nice, warm bed."

"I'm for the bed," she said, getting to her knees. "I've got jet lag and I need some solid sleep. No one will bother this field because we'll be back at dawn We'll see if there's anything in that field."

"Good idea," Nolan declared. "Don't you think there *will* be something in the field?"

"I don't know," she admitted, crawling out of the tent. As she got to her feet, she saw that the fog had moved in and the stars and moon were no longer visible. Such was the weather in England.

"We can leave everything here," Nolan told her, "except the video. We'll pack up camp after we see what's in the field tomorrow morning."

Chapter 6

Kendra received an unexpected surprise when they got back to the Michael House. Hanging on the knob of the front door was a plastic bag containing a single red rose. When she entered the foyer and turned on the lights, she found another surprise. In the bottom of the sack was Christian Campbell's business card, on the back of which he had written: "Professor, here is a gift that will keep on giving. I'd love to show you my entire collection sometime soon. I'll pick you up at noon for our luncheon engagement tomorrow. Christian."

Frowning, Kendra laid the business card on the counter in the kitchen and reached again into the sack, this time withdrawing a small green box. At that moment, Nolan sauntered into the kitchen to make a hot drink.

"Who's that from?" he asked, reaching for the teakettle.

"From Campbell."

"Again? He gave you roses earlier today."

"Stop sounding jealous, Nolan." Kendra turned and settled herself against the opposite counter from where Nolan was working. The box was leather, its green top edged with a gold border, hinting of something important inside. Excitement skittered through her as she pried open the box. A protective layer of cotton covered the object.

Nolan turned around when he heard Kendra gasp. Her eyes were wide as she held up what appeared to be a very old bronze coin. "What's that?"

"Something fantastic, I think," she answered, eyeing it critically. "This is a Roman coin. It has Emperor Hadrian's profile, and his name engraved below. And it's in beautiful, mint condition. I've never seen such a fine specimen."

Nolan came over and inspected the round coin. "May I see it?" What the hell was Campbell doing, giving Kendra something like this? Holding out a carrot? Luring her into his arms with expensive archaeological gifts? Nolan resisted voicing his opinion and took the coin from her. When their fingertips touched, those familiar tingles once again ran up his hand. How badly he wanted to hold her again!

"Is this genuine?" he demanded, turning it over and assessing it with a critical eye.

"I know it is," Kendra murmured.

"How?"

"Because I got flashes of scenes when I held it." She grinned when Nolan's brows moved upward in surprise.

"Really? What did you see?"

Kendra wrapped her arms across her body, feeling a bit defensive at Nolan's sudden interest with her psychometry. "I saw a Roman soldier. A member of royalty, a senator, in a purple woolen cap and tunic. He wore a helmet with a dyed purple horsehair crest on top of it. Purple denotes royalty. I saw a wall behind him. A rock wall about four or five feet high. I'd swear it was the same man I saw when I shook Campbell's hand. Now there's a mystery."

Nolan put the coin on the counter and continued to make the coffee, busying himself at the sink. "Where do you think this Roman leader was?" Tribunes were top dogs in the Roman hierarchy. They always came from rich, political families.

"It *felt* like Britain. Here," Kendra said, eyeing the coin.

"And that wall?" Nolan put the kettle on to boil. He then faced her as she leaned against the counter, clearly deep in thought over Campbell's unexpected and flattering gift. "Did it look like a villa foundation? Maybe one of the many forts the Romans built?"

"No, this was a wall, stretching as far as I could see on either side of him."

"Hadrian's Wall," Nolan said with finality. He pointed to the coin. "I'm a bit of a specialist in ancient coins and I'd guess that comes from here, the U.K. That type of coin was found in the middle to northern parts of this country during the Emperor Hadrian's reign. And that was when the wall was built, to keep the Celtic hordes from coming down upon them."

Kendra nodded. "You could be right. I'm not an expert in coins, but I do recognize the details of this one." The face of the Roman kept flashing in front of her eyes, which was unusual. He had a square, hard face, his eyes a glacial blue, his hair black and curled in Greek ringlets. And his build was typical Roman: heavy boned, about five foot ten inches tall and muscular. Whoever this leader was, Kendra knew he wasn't one of those rich boys from Rome who let others do his work. She saw his callused hands, his weathered features, the creases at the corners of his eyes from squinting into the sun and braving the elements. He was terribly handsome and virile, too; that Kendra couldn't deny.

"What's wrong?" Nolan asked, retrieving cups for their coffee.

"I don't know. Usually, when I put an object down, my hand stops tingling and I stop receiving pictures. But that's not happening this time. I keep seeing flashes of this Roman leader. And my hand feels like it touched dry ice."

Worried, Nolan put several scoops of coffee into a glass carafe. "Has this happened before?"

"Not ever. I can't explain it."

"Wash your hands in water as hot as you can stand, but don't burn yourself," he instructed, pointing to the sink. "That removes energy you picked up and don't want clinging to you. My grandfather taught me that little trick."

It was a good idea, and Kendra did just that. As soon as the warm water splashed across her soaped up hands, the burning sensation ceased. And so did the flashes. "They've stopped," she told Nolan as she dried her hands on a nearby towel. "Thanks. Your grandfather taught you this?"

The teakettle began to shrill. Nolan poured the bubbling water into the coffee decanter. "Grandpa Otis was a wise old codger from the Great Smoky Mountains of North Carolina. He lived on the Eastern Cherokee Reservation. He said that some things or people left behind a 'goo,' for lack of a better word, an etheric energy substance that felt sticky like glue." Setting the kettle back on the stove, Nolan added, "And when this happened you'd get certain warning signs from it, like you just experienced," he told Kendra, pointing to her hands. Graceful hands that had once loved him. It hurt to think about those times.

"A goo? What are you talking about?"

"Grandpa called it etheric dross. It's energy, but so dense you can feel it." Nolan rubbed this hands together. "If you hold an object of great power, or if a sorcerer has implanted it with his or her own etheric energy, you get a sticky sensation from handling it. And of course, if you're sensitive, you may also feel a tingling or burning."

Frowning, Kendra muttered, "I see. You said a sorcerer could implant his own energy into the object? To what end? Why would he do that?"

"Women do it, too," Nolan reminded her drily. He turned and pushed the coffee grounds down to the bottom of the glass decanter. "It's one way sorcerers mark their victims, an energetic 'hook.' They put their energetic DNA, if you will, into an object. You pick it up and, like a bacteria, get some of it on your skin. It infects you, becoming a part of your etheric field, the first layer of energy around your body. But if you quickly wash your hands in very warm water, if will rinse off, and you'll be okay."

Shaking her head, Kendra moved around Nolan. "Are you saying Campbell is a sorcerer? Or are you just jealous and concocting this story to make sure I don't go out to lunch with him tomorrow?"

Holding on to his anger, Nolan poured their coffee. He added some sugar to his cup, then walked over to the small table in the corner and sat down. "I got a bad vibe off Campbell. My birthmark burned like hell itself, Kendra. When it does that, it means I shouldn't trust the person who's setting off the alarm."

After adding milk and sugar to her coffee, Kendra sauntered over to the table. She was careful to sit as far away from Nolan as she could. "I got a similar reaction to him," she admitted, wrapping her cool hands around the warm cup.

The admission caught Nolan off guard. He sized her up. "You did?"

"Yes." Kendra sipped the coffee cautiously. "My neck takes off when there's real danger. I've had it happen in the past. I was at a dig in Italy and my neck started burning about two minutes before a wall of dirt came down on the group of people I was standing with."

"Was anyone hurt?" Nolan knew some digs could be downright dangerous.

Shaking her head, Kendra said, "No, but it taught me a lesson I never forgot. After that, I always pay attention to the warning. And whenever I do, I'm saved from injury or harm of some kind."

"Does it apply to people, too?"

She gave him an irritated look. "Yes, in my experience." He was clearly concerned. She could see shadows in his narrowed blue eyes as he studied her. Without thinking, she dropped her gaze to his mouth. Oh, what a mouth Nolan had. His lips were deliciously curved at the corners, giving him a boyish look of perpetual good humor. The crinkles at the corners of his eyes spoke of the many years he'd spent outdoors overseeing digs. It made him look even more handsome. How many times had Nolan made her laugh? Lifted her spirits when she was prone to worry?

That mouth of his could wreak an incredible fire when it roamed her body. Even now, Kendra could feel her breasts tightening, her nipples hardening at the thought of his lips upon them. Groaning inwardly, she tried to focus on the conversation and not the heated sensuality of this man she couldn't seem to ignore.

"Are you going to lunch with Campbell?"

"I don't know. First things first. I'm here to find that emerald sphere. Going out to lunch with a stranger ranks low on my priority list right now."

Relief shot through Nolan. He finished his coffee and stood up. Putting the cup in the sink, he said, "I'm glad you've got your priorities straight. For all we know, Campbell could be snooping around because he knows we're here for searching the sphere."

Kendra twisted around in the chair. "Well, if that's true, then he's *Tupay*. I remember Calen and Reno's warning that they'd tail us. He could be one of them."

"I'd give anything to lift that mane of hair to see if Campbell has the *Tupay* birthmark on his neck," Nolan muttered.

"I'll bet I could do it." Kendra grinned wickedly.

"I'm sure you could." Nolan felt a chill work

through him at her sudden suggestion. Then he saw the merriment in her wide green eyes. She was teasing him, he realized. The corners of his mouth lifted. Maybe she wasn't infatuated with the man.

"I'm going to put in a call to the foundation on our Iridium satellite phone and report on what's happened so far. You want to talk to them, too?"

"No, you do it." Kendra looked at her watch. It was near midnight. "I'm going to have a long, hot soak in my bathtub, lather up with my wonderful Herbaria orange and oatmeal soap, and then hit the hay. We're going to have to leave around four tomorrow morning to see if anything's in that east field."

Nolan agreed. How he wished he could join her in that tub. They used to bathe together and make delirious love among the soapsuds. He was heartened to hear that she still used the same organic, handmade soap as when he'd been engaged to her.

He gently pushed away the dream that would never come true, then said gruffly, "Sounds good to me. I'll set my alarm for 4:00, because I've got to get some breakfast in me before I start my day."

"Just make me some coffee and I'm set," Kendra said as he exited. She watched him disappear up the staircase.

Sitting alone in the kitchen, she found she missed Nolan's warm, strong presence. As she finished her coffee, she mentally compared Campbell to Nolan. She was wary of the large Scot with the lion's mane of thick, slightly curly golden hair, even though his rugged good looks made her drool. The man kept in excellent physical shape, too.

She needed a distraction, so she picked up a magazine from a nearby cabinet. By chance, when she flipped it open, her eye caught an ad from the Campbell Software Company. Too strange. Kendra didn't like what she saw, but it got her attention. The full-page advertisement showed a Roman soldier in a gold breastplate, in battle, swinging his short sword against Celtic warriors with blue-painted faces. Kendra had been vaguely aware of this particular software, which was adult only, due to its violence and gore. As she read the fine print, she saw that Campbell's head office was located in Edinburgh, where Christian had said he lived. And there were branch offices around the world. Most likely the man was a billionaire, because his sordid software was popular.

Frowning, she rubbed her brow and thought about the Roman coin and this violent computer game. Maybe Campbell had a fascination with Romans. When she studied the ad more closely, Kendra sucked in a breath. There in the background, behind the battling Roman tribune, the artist had painted in a white stone wall. Hadrian's Wall. Just as Nolan had said.

There was a bad taste in Kendra's mouth. She didn't like the fact that Campbell was making his billions off young children, many of whom would get their hands on this violent software game despite parental supervision. She didn't like violence being fed children through any software games, which she felt distorted their view of reality. Players would see how easy it was to kill someone, without any emotional repercussions or responsibility attached to the shocking act. Campbell's software game, which was called Roman Warrior, was all about killing, capturing and subduing. A shiver worked up her spine, and Kendra felt her birthmark burning.

Calen's words came to mind—about how a *Tupay* could be distinguished from a *Taqe* because he or she relished violence, power, control and greed. Campbell must be all of that, even if he was easy on the eyes. He supported his vision of life through his software. So what did that make him?

Suddenly, Kendra wanted nothing to do with the Scot. She didn't like his lack of morals or his treatment of the younger generation. He could have developed software that educated children and teens, but he hadn't. No, he'd chosen to highiight violence, as many other software designers did, in favor of the bottom line: making money.

Kendra left the magazine open so that Nolan would see it in the morning. After rinsing out her cup and setting it in the sink, she turned off the lights and went upstairs. Nolan's room was at the end of the dimly lit hallway. His door was closed, and she guessed he was probably in his bathroom, taking a shower. As she went into her room, she thought longingly of the baths they'd taken together. Closing the door quietly behind her, she sat on the bed and slowly untied her boots. The walls around her heart were beginning to melt, she realized.

Once she had placed her scarred boots to one side, Kendra wriggled out of her nylon trousers. Nolan's admission back at the foundation headquarters—that he'd used telekinesis to pull Debby out of the deadly grasp of the whirlpool—changed how Kendra felt toward him. As she hung up her clothes and padded naked into the bathroom, her heart felt fuller, more alive. Somehow she had a sense that the past was dissolving once and for all.

After turning on the water and adjusting the temperature, Kendra watched it flow into the large porcelain bathtub. So where did that leave her with Nolan? She was unsure, and just a little frightened of her yearning to be with him again. For all she knew, Nolan had a significant other. She wouldn't be surprised. He was a damn good-looking man who oozed charm, sensuality and heat. And if he was married or engaged or living with someone, any relationship with him would be out of the question.

Mouth quirking, Kendra put the whole emotional quandary aside. Exhaustion was eating at her. Tomorrow, they'd find out if those gold balls of light had indeed created a crop circle. Would it be the same design as in Calen's vision?

If there was some symbol marked out in the

field, Kendra was looking forward to stepping into it. She hoped it would lead her to the emerald sphere's location.

Unused to dealing with so much mysticism, Kendra stepped into the tub and settled back in the warm water. Shutting off the faucets, she picked up the pink washcloth and started soaping up. With the scent of orange blossoms surrounding her, she let her mind move back to the business at hand.

Calen had said the symbol in the field would be a step toward finding the third emerald sphere. Scrubbing her face, Kendra wondered what, if anything, the crop circle might show her. She had often stepped into ancient burial sites, some dating back thousands of years, and had picked up all kinds of scenes and impressions.

After sluicing warm water over her face, Kendra wiped her eyes with the cloth. Not only would she see temples and statues, she'd often see people wearing the fashions of different times and ages. Sometimes she'd see common scenes—women buying food in a market, a farmer riding a donkey, a warrior speeding along in a chariot. Kendra never knew what she'd find, but always, as the dig expanded, evidence of the scenes she'd envisioned would come to light. Weapons, coins, paintings, broken pottery, jewelry, vases or carved stones— they would all point to the past as she'd viewed it. And Kendra never breathed a word of this gift to her colleagues. They'd have kicked her out of that vaunted academic circle, for damn sure.

Now, however, someone wanted her gifts, needed her perceptions. A frisson of excitement thrummed through Kendra as she continued to enjoy her bath. Of course, she'd never seen a crop circle, much less stepped into one, so she didn't know what to expect. But she liked the fact that a group of people respected her talents.

As she finished her bath and wrapped herself in a fluffy pink towel, Kendra didn't feel sleepy at all. If anything, she felt like a bird dog on the scent of a quarry, her mind swimming with questions. Calen and Reno were banking on her gift of psychometry to make connection with a crop circle. Had those gold balls of light really created something in that farmer's field?

Kendra dried herself, and then brushed her hair until it gleamed. Tomorrow, she sensed, her world would change remarkably. Forever.

Chapter 7

As dawn broke over Windmill Hill, Kendra and Nolan made their way to the east field. A gray haze covered the quiet farmland, though that didn't hinder their search. And it didn't take long for them to find what they were looking for.

"Nolan! Do you see it? The symbol…it's all there!"

Due to misty conditions, Nolan had to strain to see the outlines. He and Kendra had only one pair of binoculars between them. Ragged clouds hovered in the sky, which didn't help matters. But Nolan knew they would burn off as the sun rose.

"The whole symbol? You see the concentric circles side by side?"

"Yes, both of them. This is so amazing! Here, take a look." Kendra handed Nolan the binoculars. She itched to run down the grassy hill and make her way into that field. What would the crop circle energy feel like?

"I'll be damned," Nolan breathed. "It's really there." He lowered the binoculars and glanced at Kendra. "And you caught the process on videotape. I'm glad we transmitted that footage to the foundation last night. Even if we damage or lose the actual video, they've got it stored on a computer, with several backup copies for proof. I'm sure the croppie community will jump for joy once they find out what you did."

Giving a snort, Kendra said, "I hope that tape never sees the light of day. I don't need my career ruined by having colleagues see me as a mystic or a flake."

"A shame, isn't it?" Nolan said, studying the crop circle in the growing light. "Our esteemed colleagues would deny a very rich part of every human being. We all have paranormal skills." He grinned and handed back the binoculars. "Some of us have more, is all. No one can accuse us of just having intuition. Tell me how an archaeologist knows where to dig! Long before technology was invented, it was all done by gut instinct, which worked great."

Kendra lifted the binoculars to her eyes once more and scanned the magnificent symbols in the wheat field. "I know, but I don't want to take on the whole community, Nolan. I just want to do my job."

Nolan nodded. "I think Calen and Reno will work hard to bring paranormal talents into the mainstream. As they do that, maybe we can worry less about our positions in the academic community."

The world was waking up around them, he noted. A thrush sang brightly in the woods at the base of Windmill Hill. Off to the west, he saw the dirt road they'd taken earlier. Someone was driving slowly along it, and had just doused their headlights. That was odd.

Frowning, Nolan focused his attention on the dark car, which halted a good mile away. Why would the driver turn off the lights? It was barely dawn, and headlights would be needed to see all the ruts in the road.

"We might have company," he told Kendra. "Pass me the binoculars."

Turning, she handed them over. "What do you see?"

"A car down below. Off to the west. They just turned onto the dirt road, and then doused their lights."

"That doesn't make sense," Kendra muttered. She shoved her hands into the warm pockets of her jacket. It might be June in England, but the mornings were damp and chilly. "Do you think it's a *Tupay* following us?"

"I don't know," Nolan murmured. "They've parked now, and someone's getting out."

Kendra could barely see the vehicle. She wished

for more light, but the horizon was blanketed with low-hanging clouds.

"Looks like a woman," he added. "Maybe she's lost or something."

"Could she be one of those croppies who come to the fields every day to see if any symbols have appeared? I read that they have local people checking the area daily. If they spot something, they call crop circle central and a guy in a small plane flies over and takes photos of it. There's a group nearby that is cataloging all these events."

Nolan shrugged and handed her the binoculars. "Could be. I don't know. She's looking around, so it might be a croppie doing her thing at dawn."

Kendra peered through the field glasses once again. "She looks lost. Maybe a woman from London who read about crop circles and came down here to see one? She appears to be out of her element." Kendra lowered the glasses. "Let's forget her. I want to get down to that crop circle before the farmer wakes up and finds it there."

"Yeah," he said, starting down the grassy path, "let's do some exploring. As I understand it, most local farmers aren't real happy about crop circles appearing in their fields."

Kendra fell into step at his side. "You can't blame them, though. All that flattened wheat is money he'll never be able to recoup."

"That's true," Nolan said as they descended the

hill. "But the croppie community has been raising funds to reimburse the farmers for their losses." He gestured to the field they were heading toward. "You can see how large that symbol is. It covers a lot of area. The farmer's not going to be happy to see it there."

"No, he won't, which is why I'm glad we're here so early." Kendra gave a slight grin. "I'm excited. And scared."

"Me, too. This is almost like a dig, except the evidence is scored on a wheat field instead of buried under our feet."

Eagerly, they made their way through the dark woods that ringed the base of Windmill Hill. By the time they reached the fenced field and found a gate, the light was good enough to see the crop circle. As they stopped just outside it, Kendra took in a deep breath.

"What do you need me to do?" Nolan asked. As usual, he kept his eye out for intruders. He wanted Kendra safe when she walked into that field.

"Just stay here."

"What do you do to prepare?"

"I ground myself first. And then I take a few deep, slow breaths, close my eyes and focus on my brow." Kendra touched her forehead. "At first, it's always dark, but then, if there's something significant around, it's like a screen switches on and I begin to see things."

"How long does this process take?"

"Minutes, usually."

"Do you stand or sit?"

"I usually stand, because I don't want others around me to suspect what I'm doing." She smiled wryly.

"Understandable." Nolan frowned. "But this symbol is big. Are you going to stand in the middle?"

"I've got a feeling I need to sit down cross-legged in it." Kendra pointed to the small circle to their left. "I want to head there, into the deepest part of the innermost circle."

"Sounds good to me. Let me know if you need anything from me."

"Just be a big bad watchdog, Nolan. I'll do the rest. Since I've never dealt with a crop circle before, it might take more time. I don't know what will happen, but whatever you do, don't come to touch me or talk to me. I need quiet and full concentration. Okay?" She saw the worry in his eyes. Her heart was beating a little more heavily, too, but from the excitement of what she was about to do.

"You got it. I'll stay here and be good, darlin'." Nolan gulped. He hadn't meant to use the endearment, it just slipped out. He saw Kendra's eyes widen with surprise and then sadness.

Kendra ignored the sudden tenderness in Nolan's husky tone. They had more important things to deal with. And yet she'd be lying if she said it hadn't affected her. "If some croppie comes wandering up, don't let them into the circle with me. Just ask them to wait until I leave, okay?"

"You got it." Nolan reached out and squeezed her arm. "Be careful, Kendra."

Kendra heard and felt his concern. His hand was at once firm and stabilizing. The gleam in his sky-blue eyes touched her heart, but she reminded herself that she couldn't get involved with him again. When he released her, she gave him a slight smile. "Always, Galloway. I'll see you in a few minutes." And she stepped into the circle.

Kendra's attention shifted markedly as she moved carefully through the green wheat, following the tractor's wheel ruts. She made her way toward the outer circle of the nearest symbol, trying not to trample any plants, and started to feel a little dizzy the closer she got. Continuing to take deep, slow breaths, she stepped into the first section of crop circle, and her whirly sensation seemed to abate somewhat.

Kendra worked her way across four semicircles to the area she was drawn toward. In the center was a flattened patch of wheat, the stalks all bent in a clockwise direction. Not a stem was broken, which amazed her. Sitting down, Kendra crossed her legs and rested her hands in her lap. Patting aside her fears, she closed her eyes and shifted her attention to her forehead, the point between her eyebrows.

Within seconds, she saw a flash of light, and threw her hands out to balance herself. She felt as if she were falling, and yet the screen in her mind remained dark. She had a sense of moving slowly, in a clock-

wise direction. What was happening? Was she imagining all this? It reminded her poignantly of the
whirlpool that had taken her sister's life.

That memory evoked a sudden feeling of grief and
fear within her. As much as Kendra wanted to escape
it, to open her eyes, she stayed focused on her goal.
It comforted her to have her palms pressed firmly
against the wheat around her, keeping her in touch
with reality.

The rotation became faster and faster. Kendra
sensed not only a spinning sensation but a forward
movement. And still her mental screen remained
dark. Was she picking up on the energy of the balls
of light? The whirling motion as they'd created this
symbol? What about the sense of going down a long,
twisting tunnel? Was she following the golden globes
back to their source?

While uncertain, Kendra sensed she was safe
enough. In some ways, she was like an explorer,
navigating uncharted territory. She had to follow
through on this journey, she realized. The risk taker
within her salivated over the opportunity. The human
in her, the cautious part that didn't want to die, was
equally vocal.

Suddenly, the dark screen in her mind flashed on,
and she saw rainbow hues swirling around. She was
sliding down a long, narrow tube filled with blinking,
colorful lights. The sensation of speed was even
faster now. She'd never felt anything like this before

and it scared the hell out of her. Something told her to trust what was happening, however, and she did. All her life, she'd followed her gut, and she wasn't about to ignore it now.

The details of the real world—the thrush singing, the feel of the wheat—slowly faded. As she went deeper into this endless rainbow tunnel, she sensed she was changing, shredding apart, then becoming part of something greater. Would there be any end to this, or was she losing her mind?

And then Kendra was out of the tube and standing on solid ground. When she saw where she was, she gasped.

A gleaming marble temple loomed before her, just like a scene from ancient Greece. Only this temple wasn't a historic relic. People in colored robes were climbing the wide, white steps. There was a beautiful rectangular pool in front, with yellow, white and pink water lilies floating on the calm blue water. She felt the heat of the sun above her, and yet the sky was not blue, but a pale willow-green. Where was she?

"Kendra Johnson?"

A woman's soft voice startled her. Kendra had been so drawn to the magnificent temple that she literally jumped at hearing her name. Whirling around, she saw a very old woman in a pale, shimmering robe. Her face was timeless, her mouth drawn into a smile, her gray eyes sparkling.

"Who are you?" Kendra demanded. She heard water burbling from a nearby fountain, and songs of birds she didn't recognize.

"I'm Calandra. We of the council want to welcome you to the Pleiades. You are in the star system you know as Alcyone. It is one of seven within the constellation known as the Pleiades, or Seven Sisters. I'm leader of the council. We're glad that you stepped into our circle." Gesturing to a white marble bench nearby, Calandra added, "Please, sit down, Kendra. There is much to tell you. Things that you must know before you return to your home."

There was something so loving and warm about the aged woman that Kendra instantly trusted. Sitting down, she scanned the area. "I feel like I'm in the Garden of Eden."

"Ah, yes. Well, if human beings had a million more years of evolution, your Earth might be like this someday." Calandra gave her a searching look. "You must understand that your planet is at a critical juncture right now. For many reasons, you have become a fearful and violent species. You are seen as a threat and harmful to all life in our universe."

"I don't understand," Kendra murmured.

"The Earth is at a crisis point," the elder stated. "And there are decisions she must make that will affect all who live upon her."

"Okay." Kendra nodded, not quite understanding

where this conversation was going. "I didn't realize a planet had a spirit."

"Everything has a spirit." To emphasize her statement, Calandra gestured to the gardens that surrounded the gleaming temple.

"How do you mean?"

"On your Earth there is a war taking place between the forces of light and of heavy energy. You call yourselves the *Taqe,* or light energy beings. The other side refers to themselves as the *Tupay,* or heavy energy beings. You have engaged in a war right now that is going to force Earth, as a spirit, to make some profound choices. As a council of light energy, we hope that the planet will make a positive choice for all, but that cannot come about unless the *Taqe* win this war. If you do, there will be an opportunity to replace fear and violence with compassion and understanding. And Earth will no longer be seen as a threat to us."

A hundred questions bombarded Kendra. She clamped her lips together and vowed to listen instead of asking them. "I'm assuming the Emerald Key necklace is a part of winning this war?"

Calandra nodded in turn. "Every planet has its own mythos, its own archetypes it works with energetically. There are sacred items on Earth that, if retrieved, will help you connect more surely with us, the Council. If worn by a *Taqe,* the Emerald Key will forge an important link with us, one that cannot be broken by the *Tupay* no matter how hard they try."

"But if you are so knowing and powerful, why does any of this have to happen? Why can't you just step in and help us?"

Calandra gave her a sad look. "We have agreed upon a noninterference directive. Those who are a part of the Council must obey it or they will be ejected it. We are evolved enough to know we cannot step in as much as we wish we could. We cannot take your free will. To do so means we would take on your karma, and that is not something we are willing to do. Each planet and its inhabitants must struggle, learn and evolve in their own time and at their own pace."

"Then why have I come here?"

"To take a message back to your foundation. This is our first contact with you. We want you to know that we are aware of your plight. We wish to let you know we are here. The crop circles we place upon Earth are a communications link, and hopefully the start of a dialogue between us."

Kendra relished in the warmth of the elder's aura. "How did I get here?" she asked her.

"The two concentric circles are the symbol we created: the Vesica Piscis. We devised this symbol as two separate circles. We had hoped people would see that tunnels detected in each one and realize it was a portal, and you did. You are sitting in the smaller circle, which has an energetic link to the second, larger one. We created a tunnel of energy, or what your scientists refer to as a wormhole—simply a passage from one reality and place to another."

"I'm familiar with the Vesica Piscis symbol, Calandra. Why didn't you put that in the field, instead?"

"Because it would have been too overwhelming to you and your aura. This way, we have lowered the energy frequency, so you could make the transit to us without danger." Calandra smiled. "I needed you coherent when you arrived, so that we could talk and you could take this message back to your foundation."

"I've got hundreds of questions for you."

Folding her long, thin hands over the gossamer fabric of her robe, Calandra said, "All your questions will be answered in good time. You are the first to be allowed to come here, so let's leave it at that for now. The *Taqe* have finally risen to a stable level as you struggle to remain centered in your hearts, and that is what has finally created access to us, the Council. I don't expect you to understand everything that is going on during you communication with us."

"So, if Calen, Reno, or anyone else sits in the eye of the Vesica Piscis, they can choose to come here? To you?" Kendra asked.

"Yes, if that is what they desire to do. We are opening up the energy field of this particular symbol for the first time so that contact with us is possible. Did you know that the seven groups who live on Earth originated from our star system millennia ago?"

"No, I didn't."

"All races come from five of our seven star systems. The other two systems in our seven-star constellation practiced heavy energy. Over a million years ago, we worked to persuade people of the heavy energy systems to choose the Light, and now we are one. However, the old *Tupay* left and settled in other constellations and spread their philosophy and belief of heavy energy across the galaxy before that shift occurred. The *Tupay* believed strongly in their way of life to this day and they are enemies of these constellations such as ourselves who want peace and light."

Kendra struggled with this information. "You're saying that, no matter what race we are, we were infected by *Tupay* and *Taqe* philosophy?"

"That's correct. And humans have free will to lean toward the light or the dark. You are at a crossroads right now."

"But we did come from your star systems," Kendra pointed out.

Shrugging, Calandra said, "Free will won the day. That does not guarantee that Earth will follow the same route as we did."

"Have we been at such a juncture before?"

"Many times. The last time was when Hitler rose to power. He exhibited the worst of *Tupay* energy. And the *Taqe* countries rose up to battle him in a fierce world war. Dolphins and whales were originally from our constellation. We placed them on earth to help raise the consciousness of all beings that live on your planet then, as now."

"And so our history is rife with these wars, from ancient times onward to today?"

"Yes. It is part of the struggle of a species to become conscious, to move into your heart chakras or choose to stay in your lower energy centers, where the *Tupay* like to live. If you move into your heart, it changes your aura frequency, Kendra. It sends out a compassionate signal that affects everyone and everything you come in contact with. And it automatically lifts those around you and helps them to heal, whether they realize it or not."

Frowning, Kendra rubbed her head, which was beginning to ache.

"Have you ever been on Earth? In physical form?"

"From time to time, we are allowed to send one of our emissaries to Earth. Masters in spirit, they were men and women who incarnated in order to help your planet raise its frequency. These people were not famous. They worked quietly for the betterment of others. There is a place known as the Village of the Clouds, and they work tirelessly to lift Earth's humanity to the Light."

"And you're saying they're among us now?"

"Yes, but they will never reveal who they are to you. That is the law of spirit—we cannot interfere. But they are around and are helping the *Taqe* right now, when they are given permission to do so."

"If that's true, what are the *Tupay* doing? Do they have outside help, too?"

"Yes, they do. Just as we are allowed to promote light energy as a way of living, the *Tupay* can also build their network of followers."

"Great." Kendra looked around. "So the *Taqe* are outnumbered."

"That is so, but the Emerald Key has awakened and called the *Taqe* to service for all. And you have responded. We can now respond."

"Will I ever get to talk with you again?" Kendra asked the elder.

"Yes, when the time is right. You may use the Vesica Piscis eye to return here to us next time. There's no need to have a crop circle handy." Calandra laid her hand on Kendra's shoulder. "It is time for you to go. The energy of our dimension is beginning to cause disruption in your auric field. Close your eyes…."

The moment Kendra shut her eyes, she felt Calandra touch the center of her forehead. The same explosion of light went off inside her head. And then, she was being transported back through the wormhole. This time she didn't see rainbow colors. Nothing but blackness in her mind's eye…

Part of her was relieved, because her head was splitting with pain. She wanted to get home. Home to where she was sitting in the crop circle. Home to where Nolan was waiting for her.

Chapter 8

"Kendra, are you all right?" Nolan grew alarmed when he saw her suddenly sag to the ground. He charged across the wheat field to where she lay, and, heart pounding, drew her into his arms. Her head sagged against his chest. Her lips were parted, her eyes closed. With shaking fingers, he felt for the artery in her neck.

Relief flooded him. She had a solid pulse. Nolan shifted her into a more comfortable position in his arms. "Kendra, talk to me." He didn't try to hide the urgency he felt.

He brushed her red hair back from her face. Her skin had leached from gold to an almost white color.

What had happened? He was dizzy from being in the crop circle and had to fight to stay coherent. When Kendra moaned and raised her hand, a rush of air escaped from his compressed lips.

"Kendra?"

Her thick lashes fluttered and her face slowly regained some of its color. Nolan waited impatiently for her to awaken fully.

Kendra sighed. Her head ached, but when as she opened her eyes and saw Nolan's worried face so close to hers, the pain began to recede. Gazing into his turquoise eyes, she found stability. When she realized she was in his arms, a sense of comfort flowed through her. She could see how anxious he was. Little did he know just how good it felt to be in his embrace. How she missed these arms, that special male fragrance of his. Slowly, Kendra came back to reality, and she realized with poignancy the yearning buried deep within her. Her intense feelings were a surprise, but she needed to keep them buried. At least for now.

"I— I'm okay, Nolan," she rasped. "But you've got to help me out of this crop circle."

Nolan could tell she wasn't completely in her body as he guided her out of the wheat field and led her to a tree, where they sat down.

"What time is it?" she asked, glancing around dizzily.

"You were in the crop circle for about ten

minutes," Nolan said. He sat next to her, his hand on her shoulder. "Your eyes are unfocused, Kendra. Are you seeing okay?"

Grimacing, she touched her eyelids with her fingertips. "I feel like I'm still there, still coming back…."

"Can you tell me what happened?" He gave a quick glance around to make sure they were alone. Dawn was still burnishing the horizon, a gold band pushing back the dark of night.

Kendra took a sip from Nolan's canteen. The cool water sluiced down her throat, grounding her. After drinking more deeply, she handed it back to him. Just sitting with her spine against the trunk of the tree helped her regain her balance. "What a trip I had, Nolan. I'm not sure I believe what I saw and heard, but let me tell you about it…." And she started from the beginning.

By the time Kendra finished, the whole sky had a pinkish glow, and many birds were singing. The world was waking up.

"What about the emerald sphere?" he asked. "Did the woman mention anything about that?"

Kendra smiled, glad to be feeling much better physically. "The oddest thing happened. When Calandra touched my brow, I went blank. But then my mental screen lit up again. I pictured the Tor in back of the Chalice Well, and saw a cave on one side. I heard Calandra tell me to go to the cave to look for the emerald sphere."

"That's great!" Nolan declared. "We have the next clue in our treasure hunt." He squeezed her shoulder. "Are you sure you're okay?"

"I'm fine now, like my old self." Kendra studied his dark, concerned features. "What do you make of what happened to me?" She got up without help, and Nolan followed.

"Provocative. I know you didn't make it up or dream it." Nolan studied the crop circle. "We need to get on the Iridium phone and pass this info directly to Reno and Calen. See what they think." He withdrew the satellite phone from his knapsack and punched in the codes of the Vesica Piscis Foundation in Ecuador. He handed the phone to Kendra and listened as she talked with Calen.

The world was wide-awake now. Birds flitted about looking for food, and he saw more cars along the main road. He glanced at his watch. It was 7:00 a.m. As he looked around, his gaze snagged on something atop Windmill Hill.

Someone was standing there, watching them. The back of his neck flared in warning. He rubbed the spot and quickly reached for the binoculars. As he trained them on the dark-clothed individual far above them, he noted it was the same woman as earlier. Was this a croppie looking for newly formed circles? Very possibly. Nolan got a look at her face as she lowered her own binoculars. She was middle-aged and stout, wore a long dark skirt and coat. Her hair was a washed-out blond, as if she'd treated it far too often. Her face was round and ruddy. Once she realized Nolan was looking at her, she spun away and disappeared over the crest of the hill.

While he had no idea who she was, Nolan tucked the woman's face away in his memory. His instincts told him she wasn't a croppie. Kendra was winding up the call, and he put the binoculars back in his pack.

She handed the Iridium phone back to him. "They're very pleased with the report," she told him. "Calen said that Mason Ridfort, the resident crop circle expert, had postulated that an alien nation might be trying to contact us. He was right."

While he tried to remain businesslike, Nolan couldn't help but notice how Kendra's red hair fell in disarray around her shoulders, framing her beautiful face. Her eyes glowed with excitement. "Well, as archaeologists, we're always looking for ancient sites," he answered. "I guess we're becoming astronomer archaeologists?" He grinned.

"Ad astra," Kendra said. "A Latin phrase for 'to the stars.' And yes, I think we have just broadened our careers into a brand-new frontier, where archaeologists have never gone before." She grinned back, enjoying the idea of being the first to make such a contact.

Nolan nodded and glanced at the crop circle. "Yeah, truly, to the stars. I've been thinking about your journey to the Pleiades." He pointed to the first, smaller circle. "If they designed a wormhole, as the woman said, you must have gone from the small circle to the larger circle, energetically speaking. A part of you, anyway."

"My astral form did, according to Calen. She said that when we travel to the other dimensions, it's our astral body. And when we leave, our physical body can't move, and feels paralyzed. That's how I felt, Nolan. It was as if my body had turned to stone, and I was elsewhere. The sensation was odd, but I remember any number of times waking up and feeling the same inability to move for a moment or two."

"Now I know why *I* feel that way," Nolan said.

"Doesn't it bother you that we're being watched by aliens?"

"Well, according to what Calandra told you, we're all star people, genetically speaking. Just different cultures from the Pleiades constellation." He studied Kendra's eyes as she thought about the implications. "Does that discovery bother you?"

"I don't know. There's so much to deal with here. I don't know about this law of them being able to help us only so much."

"Look at it another way," Nolan said. "People on Earth are like willful, immature children in comparison to those who live in the Pleiades. If they have a million-year head start on us, that would make sense. If you're a parent, do you always protect your children? The only way a kid learns is by making mistakes. You can't teach a child not to touch a hot stove. They have to experience it. You reinforce it with words, but kids have curiosity." He smiled. "I see this contact as incredibly hopeful. Their council has finally touched base with us. I find that exciting."

"I knew you'd see only the positive side of things, Nolan." Kendra eyed him warily.

"Hey, it's my Irish ancestry." He laughed deeply. "But I have a million questions for Calandra."

"Such as?"

"Well, what star system did Caucasians come from? Which is the African people's star system? Or other races?"

"Calandra said we didn't have much time to talk, and she had important things to tell me on this first contact."

Scratching his ear, he said, "And to realize that whales and dolphins were originally from the Pleiades, placed here as guardians to help us, well, that makes a lot of sense. The brains of those two mammals are far larger than our human one. I've always felt that they were here to help us in some mysterious way. Now, Calandra has proved my hunch."

"I love whales and dolphins, too," Kendra said softly. "Every time I see them, either in a movie, on television or in real life, I get choked with joy."

"Me, too." Nolan met her tender green eyes, then reached out and gently brushed his fingers along her cheek. Maybe he shouldn't have, but the expression

Kendra gave him was so warm and beckoning, he couldn't stop himself. He ached to lean forward and move his mouth slowly across her parted lips. And as his fingers grazed her flesh, he saw those eyes flare with surprise…and heat. He'd seen that so often when they were engaged.

Startled, he quickly withdrew his hand. He was going to apologize for touching her, but stopped himself. Because he *did* want her. All of her. There was no sense in denying that Kendra was still part of his heart.

Just then, her cell phone rang. The musical tones broke the sizzling tension building between them. He watched as Kendra pulled the phone from her pack.

"Hello?"

"Kendra? This is Christian. I hope I'm not calling you too early?"

Giving Nolan a quick glance, Kendra walked several feet away. "Why, no, I'm up and moving around." Her heart did funny flip-flops. Christian had a very low, almost growling tone, its Scottish burr sensual.

"Good lass! I'd like to bring lunch to where you're staying. I'm assuming we're still on for lunch? Did you get my roses and the interesting gift I sent with them?"

"Yes, I did. I've just been too busy to call you back and thank you."

Christian laughed. "Not to worry! I know you're

a famous archaeologist with a busy itinerary. What did you think about the Roman coin?"

Kendra glanced over her shoulder. Nolan was shrugging on his pack, a scowl on his face. He knew who her caller was. "It was in mint condition. Where did you get it?"

"Along Hadrian's Wall. I'm a bit of an amateur archaeologist, as I told you. I've done a lot of digging around Britain, and over the years have found some interesting objects. I'd like to bring some by for you to look at today while we have lunch. I've also done some excavation where crop circles appear, and have made some fascinating discoveries. Are you interested in crop circles?"

"Yes, I am."

"I'll bring what I've discovered about them, as well. Are we on for an archaeological lunch of sorts, then?"

The lure of Roman artifacts was just too much for Kendra to refuse. Plus she was intrigued to hear what Christian knew about crop circles. "Meet me at the Michael House. Do you know where it's located?"

"Of course. Across the street from the beautiful and mystical Chalice Well. I'll have my driver drop me off at noon, lass. Is that all right with you?"

"Perfect," Kendra said. "See you then."

Christian Campbell liked to stalk *Taqe* who didn't have a clue who he really was. Victor Guerra, his master, often sent him on jaunts around the world to infect *Taqe* women. Christian knew his manly good looks, the sensuality that oozed from him like honey out of a comb, always triggered a strong reaction. Usually his victim went to bed with him, blindly and willingly.

He had other skills, besides seduction. Hypnosis worked if the woman allowed him to look directly into her eyes. He could capture her spirit, and she'd be powerless to resist him. Christian liked the fact that she became a slave to his orders.

As he sat in the back of his black Rolls Royce, his driver moving slowly through downtown Glastonbury, Christian smiled to himself. It amazed him how many *Taqe* didn't realize their true identities. He found that odd and surprising. But then, through Guerra and his teachings and training, he knew each *Taqe* had to awaken to an inner awareness of self as they gradually opened their heart chakra. Then they slowly became cognizant of their enemy, the *Tupay*.

Was Kendra Johnson still ignorant of who and what she was? Christian hoped so, because if that was the case, he had a chance to infect her and disable her *Taqe* skills. Christian had to have sex with her. Once his sperm spilled into her body, she'd be rendered useless to the *Taqe* movement.

Looking out at the busy streets of Glastonbury, Christian frowned. If Kendra insisted he wear a condom, his plot wouldn't work. Unless he raped her, and that wasn't out of the question.... Christian didn't care for that method, however. His charm, his use of hypnosis, combined with charisma and sensuality, had always netted him his target. She became a willing partner, and he could defuse her as a threat.

Something told him that, with time and patience, he could lure Kendra Johnson to him. She was very interested in his coins and the crop circle information.

Christian was glad he'd sent Daria Whitcomb out to spy on the twosome this morning. The blond *Tupay* woman had been unhappy at having to climb the hill so early. Still, Daria was under Christian's command, and she followed his orders even if she hated getting her feet wet and muddy during the demanding climb.

Smiling, he noticed the high stone wall that surrounded Chalice Well up ahead. Made of the same colorful rockwork, the Michael House stood on the right side of the road. No *Tupay* could enter the garden, for it was a sacred place for *Taqe*. However, that did not apply to the house across the road.

His driver braked, put on the turn signal and pulled into the small parking lot near the two-story house. Christian carefully reined in his power. If Kendra knew who he was, she wouldn't allow him to kiss her, fondle her or take her to bed. Instead, she'd try to milk him for his information, and play the game that was always played between enemy camps. The old saying—that one kept one's friends close, but one's enemies closer—applied here. If Kendra Johnson was a trained *Taqe,* she'd try to manipulate him, just as he intended to manipulate her.

Christian thoroughly enjoyed any kind of combat. But he kept the dangers in mind. The idea of losing left a very foul taste in his mouth.

As his driver got out of the Rolls to open the door for him, Christian maintained his warrior's wariness. A Roman emperor from a very rich family, he'd learned cunning through politics, as well as through war. And he'd kept his edge for nearly a thousand years. He wasn't about to lose it now. No, he'd approach Dr. Kendra Johnson very carefully and use his abilities to see if she was awake or not.

The hunt was on!

Chapter 9

"This is an incredible coin collection," Kendra told Christian Campbell. They sat at the table in the kitchen. Holding up a small box with a glass covering, Kendra gazed in awe at the several bronze sesterces it held, each bearing the profile of Emperor Hadrian. "These are magnificent! I've never seen a collection in such mint condition."

Christian couldn't help but smile. If only Kendra knew she was talking to the man whose head was on those sesterces. As he adjusted his red-and-white striped tie, he tried to sound humble. "My love of all things Roman."

Kendra nodded and eagerly looked at the other

four small boxes that contained other Hadrian coins of the Hadrian era. "I can see you do. Most amateur archaeologists have a favorite age or century."

Campbell had arrived at noon with a picnic lunch. They had feasted upon goat cheese, grapes and multigrain bread. Christian had served her a red wine from his Italian vineyards. He owned a large villa in Tuscany and his winery produced several award-winning labels.

Kendra tried not to be affected by the power that swirled around Campbell. He was a large man, and his gold-brown eyes danced with such vitality it was tough not to be drawn to him. As she peered closely at the last set of coins through her magnifying glass, she noticed that the bronze sesterces had Hadrian's profile on one side and on the reverse, a Roman warship with oars and rowers. "These are quite remarkable," she whispered. Looking across the table, she asked, "These are part of your private collection and not from a museum?" She knew that any curator would die to have them.

Campbell shrugged. "I have a museum of sorts at my home in Edinburgh. Perhaps you'd like to come take a look at it someday? You'll see why I'm not loaning these items to another museum."

There was no missing the glint in Campbell's eyes. He wanted her. Occasionally, he would reach across the table, his large, hairy hand brushing hers. Well, she was old enough and wise enough to see the not-so-subtle sexual game going on. But she couldn't figure out why Campbell had come after her so aggressively. As one of the world's top archaeologists, Kendra frequently rubbed elbows with wealthy men who were amateur "archeo-hunters." She sensed that Campbell wanted something more from her, and she couldn't define what it was. Because of that, she remained guarded.

Of course, Nolan didn't trust Campbell and had begged Kendra to be careful around him. But as much as she tried to spot a *Tupay* symbol on the back of Campbell's thick neck, she couldn't because of his gleaming mane of hair.

"Oh, I can't go right now," she told Campbell, setting the last of the boxes of coins to one side. She popped a grape into her mouth and added, "I have other responsibilities on this trip, and I'm on a tight schedule, Mr. Campbell."

"Do call me Christian."

She nodded. "Of course, Christian."

"Why are you here, Kendra? What brings one of the foremost archaeologists in the world to sleepy little backwater Glastonbury?"

Nolan had warned her not to reveal their itinerary to anyone. She considered her words carefully as she relished the last bite of goat cheese. "There's a crop circle workshop this weekend. I have an interest in their symbology."

"Ah," the Scot said, "that makes sense. But I've

read all your articles and you've never mentioned crop circles specifically."

Kendra could feel his subtle probing. The man was absolutely mesmerizing. And if she'd been a younger woman without worldly experience, she'd have been taken in. But she was not. "It's more of a personal interest related to work, Christian, so I wouldn't have mentioned the topic in my standard articles."

"Of course. So what do you think causes these crop circles?"

Kendra shrugged and said, "I really don't know."

"There is evidence of such circles throughout history, but I'm sure you're already aware of this."

"Yes, I am." Kendra decided to turn the tables on the well-dressed Scot. "What are your thoughts on them, Christian?" she asked with a smile. She watched his ruddy features grow thoughtful as he considered her question.

"I have narrowed it down to two possibilities, Kendra. One is that these are symbols manifesting from the Earth herself. I consider Earth, or Gaia, a living, sentient being. This may be her language, and she's trying to communicate with us thickheaded humans." He tapped his finger on the table. "Or, an even more remote possibility, aliens are putting them here to try and speak with us, perhaps. I realize this second one sounds far-fetched."

"Hmm," Kendra said. "Interesting."

"What is your theory about them?"

"That human beings are out there at night with boards and ropes, making patterns that other folks will see and discuss the next morning."

"Oh."

Kendra could hear a note of disappointment in Campbell's voice. She felt it from him, even though his features never changed. "I'm a scientist, Christian. I deal with facts. A number of crop circles were made with boards."

He straightened in the chair. "But many were not. Some of those beautiful and intricate patterns couldn't possibly be made by us. Don't you think?"

Kendra paused before she answered. Again, she could feel some unidentified energy probing the outer shield around her aura. Was Campbell doing this? If so, was he aware of it? It felt like an assault to her, and she began to understand Nolan's worry about this man. He *could* be an agent of Guerra, the master sorcerer.

Kendra pushed away the unease that came with this thought, and flashed a bright smile. "I'd love to speak with you longer, Christian—" she glanced at her watch "—but I have an appointment with my colleague now. Perhaps we can stay in contact by e-mail?"

He frowned. "Well, of course. But I'd hoped to invite you to dinner at my town house here in Glastonbury tonight."

"Oh, I'm sorry, I can't do that. Thank you for the invitation, but my schedule is full."

"That's too bad…." In that instant, Christian looked into her eyes and summoned the power to hypnotize her. It had to be done. Now. Kendra's eyes widened and her pupils grew large and dark. She jerked back and then sat very still.

He had her!

Fully aware that Galloway was only a room away, Christian remained cautious. Slowly, he shifted closer to her.

"Kendra," he whispered seductively, so only she could hear him. He leaned over her shoulder, his lips near her ear. "I want you to stand up, put on your coat, bring your briefcase and follow me out the door. Do it now." If nothing else, he was going to see what papers and notes she held in that case. Some knowledge was better than none.

Stepping away, Christian crowed inwardly when she pushed back from the table and stood.

"We're going for a drive," he informed Galloway, blocking the entrance to the kitchen.

Nolan lifted his head from his reading and frowned. "What?"

"Kendra and I are going for a short drive. I'll bring her back in about an hour."

Warning signals screamed through Nolan. The Scot seemed relaxed, but stood like a bulwark in the doorway so Nolan couldn't see what Kendra was doing. He caught a glimpse of her putting on her coat and then picking up her briefcase. Her movements were…wooden. Something was wrong. Terribly wrong.

"Move aside, Campbell," Nolan growled as he got to his feet. He eyed the distance between them.

"What for?" Christian asked with an easy smile. "I think Doctor Johnson can take care of herself.

Nolan stiffened. "Kendra?" he called loudly enough for her to hear as she walked toward the back door.

"Kendra!"

She didn't stop.

What the hell was going on? Nolan wasn't sure, but his neck burned. And the cocksure smile on Campbell's face made him even more angry. He could sense some kind of showdown was about to happen. As Campbell put his hand in the pocket of his camel hair coat, Nolan knew he had to act fast. He marshaled his telekinetic powers and pointed his index finger at the big Scot. In a second, the room flashed with light, as if a bolt of lightning had struck.

Campbell yelped as he was thrown backward into the table. It collapsed beneath his weight, and the Scot crashed to the floor. Wood splintered and flew in all directions.

Breathing hard, Nolan glared at him as Campbell scrambled to his feet. Kendra was at the door, shaking her head. Turning, she gave him an odd look of confusion.

"Nolan? What's going on?"

"Didn't you hear me call you?" he demanded, moving forward to grip Campbell by the collar of his expensive coat.

"No. What happened?" She looked down at herself and the briefcase in her hand.

"I don't know. This jerk said you were going with him. Were you?" Nolan rasped.

"No, I told him I couldn't…." Kendra moved to the wall and slumped.

That confirmed it for Nolan. He wasn't as big as the Scot, but his protectiveness toward Kendra gave him more than enough strength to send the man flying across the room—with a little help from Nolan's telekinetic skills.

Kendra's mouth dropped open when Campbell slammed into the door. The glass shattered. The Scot cursed and fell to his knees. Turning, he glared at Galloway, who stood like an angry bull, glaring back at him.

"I won't forget this," Campbell snapped. He quickly got to his feet. Obviously the hypnotic spell he'd cast upon Kendra had been broken by whatever Galloway had done. Christian narrowed his eyes on the lanky Irishman. Just what the hell *had* Galloway done to him? He felt as if he'd been hit with a truck. Every bone and muscle in his body ached.

"Kendra, get over here," Nolan ordered tightly. "Move away from Campbell. *Now.*"

For once, Kendra didn't argue. His voice, the murderous look in his eyes, told her this was serious. She gripped her briefcase and moved quickly across the kitchen.

"Now leave, Campbell. And we don't ever want to see you again. Next time, you won't walk away. Understand?" Nolan growled.

Shaken, the Scot jerked the door open and hurried out of the house. He'd underestimated Galloway completely. The man was definitely a Warrior for the Light. But whatever power he had, it was one Christian had never encountered before. Bruised, his ego smarting, he hurried to his Rolls Royce. Guerra would have to know about this. About this man's unexpected and dangerous powers.

Kendra set down her briefcase and shed her coat. Nolan was on his knees with a dustpan and brush, scraping up the shards of glass on the floor. She looked at the destroyed table.

"What are we going to tell the owners about this?"

"I don't know," he groused. "We'll think of something." Glancing up at her, he asked, "Are you okay?"

"Of course I am."

"You weren't minutes ago. Campbell was taking you someplace. Do you remember where?"

Kendra rubbed her brow. "No."

"What's the last thing you remember?"

"I told him I couldn't go with him."

"What did he do to force you to go, then?"

She shivered. "He…he looked at me. In a funny kind of way. That's the last thing I remember."

"He probably hypnotized you, Kendra. Remember what Calen said—the *Tupay* have paranormal skills. Maybe Campbell's is hypnosis."

Getting up off his knees, Nolan emptied the glass into the trash. He fought the urge to go over and hug Kendra. After what she'd been through, he didn't want to confuse her more. He looked out the window, glad to note the Rolls Royce was gone. For good, he hoped. Turning, he walked back across the kitchen and shut the door.

Kendra looked up when he approached her. "What did you do? Campbell's nearly twice your size. I saw him fly backward and land in a heap in the middle of that table."

"I used my telekinetic powers," Nolan answered.

"Helluva power," she stated drily.

"I can kill with it, Kendra. It's not something I use often, and I summoned just enough force to put him at a disadvantage. When I challenged him, he put his hand in his pocket. I saw something, maybe a gun, and knew I had to stop him. You were acting funny. Wooden. Didn't you hear me call you?"

She shook her head. "No, I didn't." Glancing around the messy kitchen, she added, "Come on, let's get this cleaned up. We have to report it to the owner and get that window replaced."

Nolan was glad to have something to do. The telekinetic energy swirled powerfully within him. It would take hours for him to settle down and for it to ebb away. He noticed Kendra watching him.

"Thanks for saving me from Campbell."

"At least this time I was able to protect you," he muttered as he walked away.

"You'll get another chance when we get to that cave," she promised.

"So, what are we going to find here?" Nolan growled under his breath. He and Kendra stood in the cave beneath the Tor. They'd removed a number of wooden planks covering the entrance. It had taken them all afternoon to locate it and then get into the dank, dark hole.

Looking around with his flashlight, Nolan could see sleeping bats hanging from the cave roof, their wings wrapped around their brown bodies. In places, water dripped from the rough limestone. He was glad he and Kendra had rain jackets on.

The main part of the cave was about seven feet high and, if not for their flashlights, totally dark. "I have no idea," Kendra replied. When she heard the trickle of water nearby, she realized it must be the spring that would eventually find its way to Chalice Well, which was just below the Tor. The "red" stream, renowned for its feminine energy.

Finding a flat rock, she sat down and turned off

her light. "Let me sit a moment and see if I pick up anything."

"Right." Nolan switched off his own flashlight and quietly stood nearby. The chilling dampness was stirred by a slight air current. The steady dripping from the rocks continued. He understood Kendra needed silence, but the incident with Campbell still agitated him. And the further they got with this assignment, the more dangerous it would be. Not to mention what working with Kendra did to him. It was impossible, having a relationship with her, he knew. But that didn't stop his stupid heart from pining away for her.

Still jumpy, Nolan stayed on high alert in case of danger. Was Campbell still around?

Kendra drew several long, steadying deep breaths. This time, she was literally sitting on her subject. She opened herself up to receive information, pictures and sensations that would help them find the emerald sphere.

Closing her eyes, she visualized tree roots wrapping gently around her ankles, then stretching deep into Mother Earth. Hands resting on her damp knees, she sank more deeply into her relaxation.

Every rock recorded information, Kendra knew, because ninety-nine percent of them had crystal within them. Quartz was a natural memory keeper. A stone could record weather, animals on the prowl, or cataclysmic events. If a human walked near it, the quartz within the rock would keep an imprint energetically, record a voice and sometimes even any conversation. And that was what Kendra was after: a permanent voice recording. One she hoped would tell her something about where the emerald sphere was located. As she sank deeper into a meditative state, she was able to detect the stone's recordings.

She heard faraway voices. At first, they sounded like grunts and vocalizations reminiscent of primitive cave people. Then there was chanting and singing. Kendra saw the lean, pale hands of a man picking up the rock. He was a Druid priest, and the ceremonial chanting was a seasonal occurrence in that cave, related to solstices and equinoxes. That made sense, because Druids paid attention to the movements of the Earth and marked them in rituals.

The dripping water from the ceiling seemed to fade as Kendra entered more deeply into her focused state. The rock had been placed on top of an altar. She tried to see the whole scene but couldn't. And then her breath hitched. A fox pelt lay across the rock. And on the red fur, the Druid placed an emerald sphere. Just like the one she'd seen in photos at Reno and Calen's condo.

Heart pounding, Kendra saw the emerald sphere gleam. She felt wave after wave of energy exuding from it, like a tide of healing power. The sensations rippling through her were wonderful, and she absorbed them eagerly. As soon as the chanting was finished, the Druid picked up the sphere and slipped it into a protective leather bag. The fox pelt was then taken off the rock and folded. In its place, a woman's work-worn hands laid grain and fruit, along with acorns, a gift of gratitude, to end the ceremony.

This cave had been used in ceremonies for thousands of years, Kendra realized, by Neanderthals, and later, Celts and Druids. Other voices sounded, and she heard Latin, a language she understood, and another scene appeared. To her shock, the stone altar was being smashed with heavy iron mallets and utterly destroyed. The anger of the men she saw— Christian monks—was virulent. The entire altar was disassembled and the rock she sat upon hurled toward the back of the cave. And that was where they'd found it today.

She heard men whispering once more, speaking Middle English. She estimated they were from the 1500s. Ashes from a torch fell upon the rock that had once been the main piece of the altar. The men looked around and wondered what the cave had been used for. They left, and other male voices came through. This time, the group moved respectfully around the space. They seemed to realize this cave had once been a powerful ceremonial vault where magic took place.

Kendra waited as the images moved closer to present day. Teenagers, high on drugs, accidentally straggled into the cave. They used it as a refuge to drink beer and smoke marijuana. Then the pounding of hammers reverberated in her ears. Kendra surmised that the townspeople of Glastonbury had come and sealed the cave entrance to stop anyone from entering.

Taking a deep breath, she wondered if the emerald sphere was still around. It was not, she sensed. Another place appeared. A triangular structure built by hand upon a slight rise. At the entrance, massive slabs of rock had somehow been stood upright to form an entranceway. As Kendra shifted to one side, she saw a flight of hand-hewn, gray stone steps going down into the darkness, and she descended them. Her eyes grew used to the dim light, she noted that rooms had been built on either side of a main walkway. It reminded her of a barrow, utilized by Druids for ceremony and sometimes for burials. As she walked forward, she found her way blocked off by a wall of red bricks. Bricks were Roman phenomena, certainly not Iron Age or Druidic.

Kendra looked around and memorized everything she could. And then, the screen in her forehead went blank.

Releasing a long breath, she brought herself out of her deep state. Slowly, the sounds of the cave became clear again. She inhaled the dank air, smelled the moss that grew on the walls and heard the trickle of water behind her. Nolan moved and she heard his boots crunching against stones on the uneven floor. Opening her eyes, she blinked a few times. Nolan was standing near the passageway heading to the cave entrance. He was like her guardian in that moment, and Kendra felt his protectiveness.

"Did you see or hear something?" she asked him, her voice echoing softly in the chamber.

"What?" Nolan half turned toward her. "Did I disturb you?"

"No, I was coming out of my state when you moved. Is something wrong?"

"I don't know. I feel danger. I was going to walk back to the entrance to check on things." He didn't say it, but he wondered if Campbell was hunting them—again. Nolan didn't want to upset Kendra, so he said nothing.

"What kind of danger?" Kendra stood and dusted off her pants. She thought of the Scot, whose sinister intentions were now apparent. She wouldn't put it past Campbell to come back and finish what he'd started. The idea made her shiver.

"Just a threat, a feeling. Like someone's watching us or lurking around outside the cave." It had to be Campbell. Nolan's gut told him that.

Kendra picked up the stone and set it out near the wall. It was important, because the emerald sphere had been placed upon it. She patted it and mentally thanked the spirit of the rock for its help. Her hand tingled, as if the stone returned her silent tribute.

Straightening, Kendra made her way to Nolan's side. His profile was strong, his eyes focused toward the exit.

"Maybe kids? Or tourists? There are lots of visitors on the Tor right now."

"Maybe you're right," he said, gazing back at her. "Get anything by sitting on that rock?"

"Yes, plenty. But let's leave and put those planks of wood back in place. This cave is sacred, and people shouldn't be wandering in here. Let's try to preserve some of its energy for future generations."

When they finished the task, the sun was sinking toward the horizon. The Tor rose above them, a herd of cows munching away on the green grass that covered its steep sides. Nolan's gaze moved up at the top where St. Michael's Tower stood, all that was left of a centuries-old, gray stone church. To his surprise, Nolan spotted the same woman he'd seen that morning at the crop circle. He gripped Kendra's elbow and guided her down to the thick stand of oaks at the base of the Tor. They had to leave. Now. On the way, he filled her in on the mysterious woman.

"Do you think she's one of Guerra's henchwomen?" Kendra guessed as they tramped into the woods, heading back to the parking lot.

"I don't know," Nolan said. "When my birthmark takes off as it's doing now, I always think there's a *Tupay* tailing us. Before Reno and Calen told us about them, I'd feel my neck heating up maybe once or twice a year. Over here, it's happening all the time. But I know what's causing it. It's a warning that enemies are present."

"Makes sense," Kendra murmured. "Let me tell you what I felt, Nolan."

By the time they reached their rental car, the sun had set. Most of the tourists who'd been on the Tor were coming down the narrow walkway to the parking lot. Nolan looked around for the blond woman who had been watching them earlier, but he didn't see her. Nor did he spot Campbell, who would easily stand out because of his height and hair.

As Nolan drove them back to Michael House, he said, "I'm really impressed. I never thought anything about how psychometry worked or how useful it could be until you came along."

Kendra's cheeks flushed at the feeling of tenderness Nolan brought out in her. She knew the rock she'd sat on, and the emerald sphere she'd viewed, had somehow passed along healing energy to her. As a result, she didn't fight the warmth she felt toward him now. He was protecting her while she worked.

Maybe he was trying to atone for not being able to save her sister on that fateful day. The memory didn't have the bitterness it always evoked before, and Kendra was grateful. There was a lot about Nolan that she admired and even liked.

Still, she couldn't fully trust him. And probably never would. With the *Tupay* around and her nasty experience with Christian Campbell, Kendra wanted Nolan's protection. And he seemed able to deliver it.

His telekinetic abilities amazed her. To hear of it was one thing, to see Nolan in action, quite another.

"The new glass in the door should be installed by now," Nolan teased as they parked at the Michael House. They'd called the owner, who'd promised to have it fixed promptly.

Kendra grimaced. "I hope so. I don't want any reminders of Campbell." She got out of the rental car. The evening was cooling rapidly, the sky darkening. Most of the birds had quieted. "We've got work to do tonight, Galloway. I have to identify the barrow I was shown. It's either where the emerald sphere is located or the next step in finding it. You and I are going to scour the Internet to locate that place. It's somewhere here in England, and we have to find it tonight."

Nolan leered playfully. "Together. Now, I like the sound of that. We're a team, at last!"

Laughing ruefully, Kendra opened the door to the house and stepped inside. "You know what, Galloway? You're incorrigible."

He followed, giving her a wink as she took off her jacket and hung it on a peg in the hall. "Music to my ears… Let me stir up a mean Irish stew for us tonight, and then we'll get to work…."

Chapter 10

"This isn't going as I'd planned," Hadrian told Victor. He had given the master sorcerer a full report on his activities to get Kendra Johnson to trust him. While Hadrian's physical form rested in his town house in Glastonbury, he had traveled astrally to the Other Worlds to visit the Dark Lord.

The sorcerer sat relaxed in the black leather chair behind his desk. "Then I need to become more directly involved. If Doctors Johnson and Galloway now know you are *Tupay*, you are less effective for this mission. There may be other ways I can utilize your services."

Hadrian grimaced. "I thought this would be easy."

Victor shook his head. "It never is with Warriors

for the Light. Where is this team off to tomorrow morning? You had Daria Whitcomb follow them to that cave beneath the Tor."

"Yes, she did follow them. From what she could see, they arrived with nothing and left with nothing. Later, after dark, I drove over there and looked around the cave. And found nothing. Certainly, there was no emerald sphere or any type of energy signature to show it was there. Not that we know the signature, but a ceremonial object like that would be very easy to spot because of its power."

"Very well. I want you to follow them in something other than your Rolls Royce. Tail them, and let me know where they go. Once they park, I'll get active."

Nodding, Hadrian said, "As you will, my lord. I'm sorry I could not be of more use."

"There it is," Kendra said excitedly. It was barely dawn, and they'd just reached the Avebury stone circle. She spread a topographical map across the car hood and ran her finger from the famous ring of standing stones to the second Tor, built by Neolithic people. Then she noted the West Kennett Barrow on a rolling hill, surrounded by farm fields, about half a mile away. "Look at this, Nolan. Clearly, there's some kind of energy connection among these three. We know the ancients worked with Earth energy."

Nolan followed her finger as she pointed out the three sacred sites on the map. "You're right. They were very attuned to the Earth and her invisible energy grids. Nowadays, dowsers can follow the ley lines, which generally run east-west or north-south."

"Not always," Kendra said. "Remember, topographical elements plus rivers and lakes made ley lines bend here and there, following the landscape." She indicated the Tor, looming beyond the parking lot where they sat. The early morning was foggy, the mist an eerie opaque layer across the wet grass. The fenced-off area contained a large, broad field surrounding the manmade hill. "I believe these mounds were situated where several ley lines meet," Kendra said. "Ancient priests and priestesses were sensitive to such energy and knew where it flowed. And they built these hills to somehow take advantage of high-energy hubs or concentrations."

Nolan nodded. "No disagreement. Avebury is one of the finest prehistoric stone circles in Europe. And that barrow you saw in your vision is up on that knoll." He pointed to a slight hump on the horizon, visible above the mist. "If you ran a wooden ruler from Avebury to that barrow, you'd see that the Tor was built between them, almost at the midpoint."

"Maybe the Tor was put here to strengthen the ley line between Avebury and the West Kennett Barrow?" Kendra wondered.

"Maybe the builders wanted to take advantage of the ley line energy and situate the Tor to somehow utilize the energy."

"That's possible, too." Kendra folded up the topographical map. The fog moved slowly, white wisps drifting across the grassy field between the parking lot and the distant Tor. No one was allowed to go behind the fence. Only photos could be taken of this Tor, unlike at Glastonbury, where one could climb at will. This hill was off-limits. Why? "I suspect there's something inside this Tor, and that's why it's closed to the public, Nolan."

"The question is what?"

"The emerald sphere?"

"Maybe, but your vision was of the West Kennett Barrow, up on that hill."

"I know." Studying the landscape, Kendra realized they would have to cross a two-lane highway and then walk between two large fields, following a narrow dirt road that curved upward toward the Neolithic barrow. "Well, let's get going. We were able to identify the mound last night on my laptop. Now let's hike up there and see if the rest of my vision fits. If it does, then this is the place we were guided to, and maybe we'll find the emerald sphere."

"It won't take long to get up there," Nolan said. "And it's smart to go early before the hordes of tourist buses arrive."

"Yeah," Kendra growled. "I'm going to need some serious quiet time in there to use my psychometry. If I'm disturbed, I'll lose the connection."

"I'll stay at the barrow entrance and make sure no

one disturbs you," Nolan promised, grabbing his backpack from the car. They locked it and began their walk through the patchy fog. Up above, the barrow appeared to be nothing more than a mound of dirt covered with grass. The sky was clear, the air chilly and damp as they trotted across the highway, passed through a gate and onto the lane that would lead them to the barrow.

Kendra was optimistic as they approached the sacred site. The huge vertical slabs of gray rock looked identical to what she'd been shown yesterday in the cave. She and Nolan moved to the left and found stone steps that led down into the earth. The barrow had four chambers in it, just as Kendra had seen. The place was silent, but she felt a pulsing energy coming through the elongated mound.

"Do you feel that? The energy?" she asked Nolan, who stood behind her. "It's like invisible hands pushing me backward."

"Yes, that's ley line energy for sure," he told her. "There's usually a pushing or pulling sensation. And it pulses. Like a heartbeat, only what's being pumped is the energy of Mother Earth."

"Wonderful," Kendra said as she surveyed the two square compartments on the right side of the passageway. She pointed to the one farthest away. "That's where I'm going to sit."

"Get comfortable. I'll play guard dog and stay

outside. If anyone comes, I'll detain them until I see you come out."

"It might be a while," Kendra warned. At the Glastonbury Tor, it had taken her a good thirty minutes to receive information.

"Don't worry about it." Nolan turned to go back up the steps. "If you need help, I'll be within earshot."

"I feel safe and good down here," she said. "Like I'm coming home…."

"Maybe you had an incarnation as a Druid priestess here at this barrow?" Nolan suggested.

Kendra smiled. "Anything is possible. See you later." She moved down the hard-packed hall between the compartments.

Stepping into the space she'd chosen, Kendra sniffed the dank air, the comforting smell of the soil. Then she sat cross-legged on the damp floor. Grounding herself, she closed her eyes. Almost instantly, she felt a downward spiraling sensation. The screen between her eyebrows opened up and she saw herself going through many strata of dirt and rock. And then the movement stopped.

Perplexed, Kendra found herself in a dark space. She couldn't see anything because it was pitch-black. She waited. Nothing happened. Finally, she called out telepathically and asked for help.

"Is there something or someone I can talk to? If so, will you show yourself to me? I come in peace and I mean no harm."

Kendra shifted slowly, hoping to see even a bit of light. A hint of a shape. Anything…

And then a very thin vertical slit of yellow light opened up in front of her. Puzzled, she stared at it. The vertical strip was much taller than she was and seemed to be right in front of her.

What was she looking at? As she mentally asked the question, the glowing shape widened a bit more, and Kendra felt as if she was being watched. The bright field of yellow got larger and larger, until finally a black beam appeared on the edge.

Kendra stared hard. She'd never seen anything like this before. And then it hit her. She was looking into the eye with a vertical iris of some gigantic creature! Blinking, she gazed in awe as a dim, grayish outline appeared. It was a dragon!

Kendra's heart thudded with shock, but she forced herself to take note of every detail. The dragon was black, and as the light grew brighter, Kendra saw scales along its very long, thin nose. The dragon's head reminded her of a crocodile's, only there were small horns on top. It had rounded nostrils and enormous glowing eyes.

As a child, Kendra had read voraciously about mythical dragons…but this was the real thing. And huge! She felt tiny compared to the enormous beast curled up before her.

Gathering her courage and trying not to let shock get the best of her, Kendra spoke telepathically to the creature eyeing her.

"Thank you for being here. I'm Kendra Johnson. May I ask your name?"

Kendra watched as the dragon blinked. There was an incredible power throbbing around it, she realized. Swallowing hard, Kendra waited patiently. It was as if the dragon was deciding whether or not to speak to her.

"I'm called Eurica. I'm the spiritual guardian of this sacred site."

How did one address a dragon? Unsure, Kendra said, *"It's nice to meet you, Eurica. What exactly to you do here?"*

"I was asked by the priestesses who once cared for this place to stay and watch over it after the humans left. My job is to protect the sacredness of this temple, as well as the two lines of energies— male and female—running through it. I cleanse them four times yearly with the fire of my breath. I help keep Mother Earth in harmony by doing this."

"Oh...I see." Well, sort of…. The gray light revealed Eurica's scaled body. The spirit dragon was wrapped around the barrow, as if the sacred site were her child to protect. Her long tail was curled like a cat's about her pear-shaped form.

"I have waited a long time for you to come here. You are the one I was to speak to."

"Me?" Kendra asked mentally.

"The high priestess said you would come here from another age and time. Dragons have been slaughtered by humans, and normally we never speak

to them, but she gave me orders to speak with you when you arrived. Dragons see most humans as backward and unworthy of our attention or acknowledgment."

"Thank you for talking to me, Eurica." Kendra floundered for a moment, but felt she should get to the point. *"Do you know anything about the Emerald Key necklace? I'm here in England to try and find it."* Holding her breath, she watched the dragon blink again.

"I know where it is located. You are to go back to the Tor in Glastonbury. Below the hill there is a sacred garden. And in this garden are two very old yew trees. You are to stand between them in the light of the full moon and ask for the sphere."

Relief flowed through Kendra, and she relaxed her tense shoulders.

"Ask for it," Eurica repeated. *"It will unveil itself. Do this on the full moon two hours after the sun has set."*

She felt such gratitude toward the black dragon. *"Thank you. Thank you so much. You have no idea how grateful we are that you could help us."*

"I am charged with helping you. Now, allow me to return to my duties."

"Of course. Thank you." Kendra watched as the dragon closed her eyes. The grayish light began to ebb, and within moments, Kendra was once more in complete darkness. The whirling sensation, upward

this time, began. Soon she felt heaviness in her body, as she returned to it. Groggy, hands pressed against her face, she sat in the earthen chamber, trying to reorient herself.

How would Nolan react to her unexpected visit with a dragon? Would he laugh at her or take her seriously? She had no way of knowing until she told him this remarkable story.

When Nolan left Kendra alone in the sacred barrow, he sauntered around the massive stone front and looked down the long, sloping path to the highway. No one was around, and it was quiet. He slid his hands into his jacket pockets as he gazed out at the wheat fields. Birds began to chirp, welcoming the day. There was a slight tinge of pale gold along the eastern horizon. Even though he was checking for danger, he couldn't help but notice the natural beauty of the scene.

Nolan moved toward the gate that allowed visitors to access the barrow. He wondered what Kendra would uncover. Was the emerald sphere here? He didn't feel it, but then, why would he? He had no experience with such a unique energy.

Calen and Reno had warned them that their quest would be like a treasure hunt, with many threats to deal with. Nolan thought again of Campbell. In a satellite phone call to Reno, he'd learned even more about the man. Campbell was a billionaire who had made his fortune selling violent computer games. Nothing overtly suggested he was *Tupay,* other than his sordid career. But that was enough proof for Nolan that he was an enemy.

Rubbing the back of his neck, Nolan stepped outside the swing gate. He glanced at his watch. It was 6:00 a.m. The temptation just to enjoy the dawn was strong, but Reno's further warning that Guerra and his henchmen would shadow them kept him alert.

At about six forty-five, Nolan noticed a blue car parked in the lot below. A tall, lean man climbed out and started heading up the hill to the barrow. Simultaneously, Nolan's neck began burning. As he made his way down the wide path toward the stranger, his gut tightened. Something was wrong—wrong enough to keep him on guard.

In his early twenties, the man wore a floppy green hat over his long, reddish-brown hair. His deeply tanned face was oblong, with a strong chin, but he seemed like a tourist from the way he was dressed. It was the stranger's eyes that caught Nolan's attention as he drew closer. They appeared flat and lifeless, devoid of all light and feeling.

Nolan watched as the man came nearer. He wobbled a bit, as if drunk. Or worse, on drugs. Nolan assumed it was the latter since that would explain why his neck was burning like fire. A druggie could be dangerous, especially if on cocaine.

Grimly, Nolan stopped and took his hands out of his pockets. No way was he going to let a twenty-year-old on drugs go through that gate to where Kendra was working.

"Good morning," Nolan said warily, sizing him up.

"And g'day, sir," the young man said cheerily, in a thick Australian accent. He halted and eyed Nolan with interest.

"You coming to see the barrow?" Nolan demanded. Something odd was going on here. The young man seemed almost like an automaton, a robot. He took his time in answering.

"Why, yes, I am."

"Actually, I have a friend who is in there right now," Nolan told him calmly. "I was wondering if you might wait here until she comes out. She shouldn't be too much longer."

"Why sure, mate, not a problem." He grinned and took off his cap, scratching his uncombed hair. Then he clapped the hat back on his head and thrust out his hand to Nolan. "I'm Miles Collingsworth."

Nolan shook his hand, noting his damp palm and weak grip. "The name is Nolan," he said. "What part of Australia are you from?"

"From Perth. The southwest." He wobbled again, as if trying to keep his balance.

"That's a nice area," Nolan said. *Was* Collingsworth drunk? His speech was slightly slurred and his eyes out of focus again. Most confusing to Nolan were the Aussie's jerky movements, almost as if he were a puppet, being controlled by someone else.

"Been there, have you, mate?"

"In my travels, yes."

"You're American?"

"That's right. What are you doing here in England?"

Rubbing his stubbled jaw, Miles said, "I'm a ley line hunter."

"Really?"

"Yes. I'm writing a book about them." He waved his hand. "I'm doing research in the Avebury area right now. You know, two major ley lines come out of the ocean near Tintagel, in Cornwall. They snake around through this area and then continue north to Scotland, and back out to sea once more. Wherever these two lines flow, early tribes built dolmans, tors, stone circles or—" he waved again "—mounds like this barrow. Iron Age tumuli are also built on them."

Nolan wasn't certain why his birthmark kept burning, but he stayed focused. Miles was an unkempt character, but seemed friendly enough. Nolan picked up the scent of marijuana around him. Probably a kid kicking around Europe before he settled down, he reasoned. There were plenty who took this route in their early twenties. "So you're a writer?"

"I am. And ley lines fascinate me." He rubbed his long, thin hands together as if to warm them. "I've been all over Europe, and now my focus is on England. When I'm done here, I'm going to Wales, then Ireland. I've already traced these two lines down from Scotland to here. I came to the barrow this morning to do a little more dowsing." He pulled out two bent wires from his back pocket and showed them to Nolan.

"Dowsing?"

"Yes. My dad is a water dowser in Australia." Miles grinned. "He's got more work witching for water than he has time on this Earth." Miles chuckled indulgently. "Australia's interior isn't exactly saturated with it."

Nolan watched as he handled the bent hanger wires. He seemed to know what he was doing. He faced south and slowly moved the L-shaped rods toward the barrow. Both suddenly veered left, indicating they'd found a different energy.

"See? I did a lot of work on this barrow the last week, and this morning, I was going to finish off my notes and do just a little more snooping around before I meandered on to the Glastonbury area. You know, the two leys go right through the Tor there, through Chalice Well, and link up with the Avebury complex here?"

"I didn't know that," Nolan murmured. He glanced over his shoulder. Kendra had just appeared. "My friend is done. I'll walk you up," he offered.

Miles nodded and stuffed his trusty dowsing rods

back into his pocket. "Thanks, mate. Looks like your sheila is done with her meditation."

Kendra wasn't exactly his "sheila," but Nolan didn't correct him as they walked shoulder to shoulder up the path. On their way, they saw Kendra coming out the gate toward them. Nolan had to restrain himself from running to her. As she drew closer, he searched her face. She seemed tired and slightly dazed; probably still coming out of whatever energy she'd contacted, he guessed.

"You find anything in there?" Miles asked her eagerly as she halted before them.

Nolan introduced the two. Collingsworth suddenly seemed very interested and fully focused on Kendra. Her brows rose a bit at this stranger's avid appraisal of her.

"No...not really," Kendra she, smiling slightly. "I just love to meditate in sacred places."

"Mmm, that is definitely a sacred space," Miles agreed. "Did you make contact with anything in there?"

"Like what?" Kendra asked, slipping her hands in her coat pockets. Clearly, she felt wary as Collingsworth crept closer. She took a step back.

Miles waved toward the barrow. "You know the Druids worked with dragons. Fire-breathing types. They say there's a dragon in there." He held up his dowsing rods for Kendra's inspection. "My rods say there is, but I've never been able to connect with it."

"Dragons?" Nolan asked skeptically, then caught

her look of unease. Without a word, he grasped her arm and placed himself between her and the stranger. His protective move made Miles scowl, take a step back. What was this guy up to?

"Sure, mate. If you dig deep enough into the mythology, you'll find dragonkind are connected with the four elements and with energy lines." Collingsworth stared hard at Kendra, who stood close to Nolan. The Aussie's gaze raked her, and he seemed very interested in the pockets of her jacket. "Their job is to keep the ley lines clean and clear for our old mother here," he added, gesturing toward the ground.

"How would they do that?" Nolan asked. He was stalling for time. The man wanted something from Kendra. For her sake, Nolan had to get them away from this guy.

Mentally, he summoned his telekinetic energy. It awakened at once, swirling through him, then into his right hand. His fist throbbed with the leashed power, which came from Mother Earth.

"Fire. It's all going to be in the book I'm writing," Miles said, still peering toward Kendra. "Archeologists have found huge middens of charred wood, where bonfires occurred over time. And if you map these heaps of charcoal, you see they follow the ley lines exactly. My hunch is that the Druids, and even the people before them, built huge fires on solstices and equinoxes. They happened in unison, on the same day and time, all across Great Britain. Fire is a great cleanser. These ley lines are like circulatory vessels for Mother Earth. The pagans knew to build wood pyres twenty or thirty miles apart, all along these leys, to keep the energy flow moving. A clean ley line makes for a happy Earth, and everything stays in harmony. The Druids were doing yearly housecleaning, if you will."

"All of this is very interesting. When is your book coming out, Miles?" Nolan asked.

Kendra was thankful Nolan was serving as a wall between her and this highly disturbing man. And yet his information was important. He'd mentioned a dragon at the barrow; well, there was one. Not that she was going to tell him about her experience. Collingsworth might know something that could help them, however, so Kendra tried to appear relaxed.

"Oh—" Miles laughed "—whenever I get done tripping around the world to find other ley lines and sacred areas connected with them, I'll settle down and write the book. I haven't even thought of a title as yet."

Lifting his hand, Nolan said, "Well, it was nice meeting you, Collingsworth. We have to get going now."

Miles frowned. "Can't you stay and talk more? I'd like to know about what you're doing—"

"We have to get going," Nolan almost growled easing Kendra ahead of him down the path. "Good luck studying the barrow up there. Goodbye."

Miles shrugged. "G'day, mates. Nice talking with you." He turned and with long, lanky strides followed the path toward the barrow.

Nolan kept Kendra moving down the path toward the car below. Every once in a while, he'd glance back to make sure Collingsworth was heading away from them. He was. Relieved, Nolan willed the telekinetic energy to withdraw. He waited until they were out of earshot to talk with Kendra.

"You all right? You look like you've blown a fuse or something." He grinned at her, wanting to buoy her spirit a little.

Kendra pushed her hair away from her face. "I went really deep, Nolan. Far deeper than I've ever been before." She glanced over her shoulder, to see that Miles had made it to the gate. "What an odd synchronicity," she said. "And what a weird man that was. Did you know him?"

"No. In fact, I felt threatened by him. I don't know why. My birthmark burned, which was all the warning I needed. He seemed too damned interested in you."

"I know. Why me?"

"You're a good-looking woman."

Snorting, Kendra said, "I didn't feel that from Collingsworth. He wanted something else. It was a strange sensation."

"I suspect he was high on drugs, saw a good-looking woman and wanted her. Plain and simple."

Nolan hoped she would just accept this explanation. She didn't need to worry any more than necessary.

"Galloway, you're such a Neanderthal at heart."

"Hey, survival of the fittest." He chuckled, some of the tension draining from him. He looked back one last time and saw that the Aussie had disappeared over the hill. Most likely, he was inside the barrow doing his thing. Nolan cupped Kendra's elbow and urged her toward their rental car. It would be a helluva lot warmer than standing out in this damp, cool air. "Can you tell me what happened when you were in the barrow?"

Kendra allowed him to keep his hand on her. The contact was stabilizing, and right now, she wanted it. "I'm not sure *I* believe what just happened to me in there."

"Can it be more weird than going to the Pleiades in that crop circle?" he teased.

Kendra frowned. "I guess not, now that you mention it."

"What happened?"

"I have to tell someone. This is just too strange," she said, rubbing her brow. "I—I saw a black dragon wrapped around the barrow, Nolan."

He gripped her arm tightly as they reached the highway. There were no cars in sight, so they hurried across to the parking lot. He opened the car door for Kendra and she slipped in.

"A dragon?" he said thoughtfully, standing there with his hand on the open door. Looking toward the barrow, he said, "That's funny. Miles was talking about dragons. He said there was one in there, but he couldn't contact it. He'd discovered it through his dowsing rods."

Relief funneled through Kendra. She placed her hand on her heart. Nolan wasn't making fun of her. That was important. "I thought I was imagining the whole thing. I thought I'd gone over the edge."

Nolan got in the driver's side and closed the door. He turned the engine on and got the heater working. The worry on Kendra's face pained him. He wanted to assuage her anxiety.

"Tell me about it! I'm all ears."

Chapter 11

The instant Victor Guerra exited Miles's body, the young man sagged to the ground on the path next to the entrance of the West Kennett Barrow. Dead. In his spirit form, Victor snickered over the ploy. It had worked as usual; the two Warriors for the Light were ignorant as hell about who'd inhabited that youth's drugged body. Actually, it was simple for a *Tupay* to enter a substance abuser, whose aura was usually full of holes, the normal protection mechanisms no longer in place. Miles Collingsworth had been easy prey.

Congratulating himself on a job well done, Victor followed his quarry's car. If he slipped into the vehicle to listen, he knew both would feel his presence, and they'd stop talking.

That was critical, knowing when to listen and when not to. It had taken Victor many lifetimes to get it right. Galloway had sensed his presence in the airliner, and that had been a warning to Victor. But in a car, there was no room to maneuver. So he'd have to be patient, which was not his strong suit. Even after four thousand years, he realized, he still had not learned that lesson.

Absorbing the information about the black dragon guardian at the West Kennett Barrow, Victor was not surprised over the discovery. He'd picked up on Eurica's vibrations when she'd unveiled herself. Thousands of years ago, he'd seen them flying in the skies over Europe and China. It was during the Dark Ages that the dragons had been wiped out. Because the dragon nation was *Taqe* by orientation, Victor steered clear of them. He didn't grieve over their slaughter by the stupid Europeans, who thought of them as the devil's henchmen. Fools that they were, they did not realize the service that dragons performed for the health of the Earth. The Dark Ages had been a time of blind ignorance, in his opinion.

As he followed the two archaeologists back to Glastonbury, Victor smiled. That black dragon must have known something. He hoped it had imparted knowledge of the emerald sphere's location. Worriedly, Victor glanced back toward the barrow one last time. The black dragon's main task was to guard the site. Still, Victor understood enough about the creatures to know that once they deigned to make contact with a human, a connection was forged. Would that female dragon stay put when he attacked the warriors to get that emerald sphere? That was a very real concern to Victor. He might be a master sorcerer, but dragons were thirty times larger, and every bit as powerful.

Victor could not ignore the niggling threat that this great black being might leave her post to protect Dr. Johnson. A dragon's fiery breath could cause real harm to anyone, whether in physical form or not. Victor had no desire to be incinerated in that way. A dragon's fire could be fatal even to an immortal.

Victor needed to know what the warriors were discussing. Now. It about killed him to remain discreetly behind the speeding car, but all he could do was wait—and watch.

"This is bizarre," Nolan confided to Kendra as they sped toward Glastonbury. "I wonder how our next satellite phone report to Calen and Reno will sound. 'Oh, by the way, Kendra ran into a black dragon guarding the barrow. Her name is Eurica, and she's given us a lead in our search for the emerald sphere.'" Nolan grinned.

"Somehow," Kendra said, "I suspect they will take

it in stride. I believe they know a lot of things they're not telling us because we're scientists, not mystics."

"Yes. Mystics do live in their own realm, don't they."

Shaking her head, Kendra said, "I don't know why Eurica said to wait until the next full moon to go to those two yew trees in the garden at Chalice Well. Why a full moon?"

Nolan enjoyed their easy conversation. Kendra was relaxed now, and their banter reminded him of long ago. This kind of sharing with her was food for his starving soul. "The full moon means fruition. That's the time a seed will pop out of the ground and begin to grow. From an astrological perspective, it means something is ready to emerge or bloom."

"Hmm, that may make sense," Kendra murmured, thinking about it. "Eurica said to stand between the two trees and ask for the sphere to appear." She turned and studied Nolan's profile as he drove. "Is it possible this sphere is not in our dimension?"

"I don't know. Maybe we'll get insights from Calen and Reno about Eurica's instructions. I thought all the spheres were in this reality, hidden right here on Earth."

"But maybe they're not." Kendra sighed and eyed the tall hedgerows alongside highway. The landscape in southwest England was mostly agricultural, the roadways narrow. It wasn't a relaxing drive, especially when a wide truck came zooming toward them over the center line.

"Let's see what Calen and Reno think," Nolan said, deftly avoiding the truck and speeding on toward the guesthouse.

Later that morning, Kendra told Calen and Reno about the dragon's message. As she spoke on the phone, Nolan sat opposite her, on the living room couch.

"I don't know what to say, Kendra. We need to contact Grandmother Alaria and Grandfather Adaire at the Village of the Clouds for more information," Calen stated. "Like you, I thought the emerald spheres were third dimensional. Why would one not be? What does that mean?"

"Is it possible I made up this whole thing regarding the dragon and what she told me?"

"No. Ana Ridfort just got back from a week of training at the Village of the Clouds. She's listening in on your report. Let me put her on the phone with you?"

"Sure…"

"Kendra? Hi, this is Ana speaking. We haven't met in person yet, but it's nice to talk to you."

"Same here, Ana. What's your assessment of this spirit dragon and the info she gave to me?"

"Well," Ana said, "Grandfather Adaire just taught me about some of the spirit guardians the *Taqe* work with. Dragons aren't originally from Earth. He said that the constellation Draco is their real home. But dragonkind are of the Light. They have quietly seeded themselves in many different galaxies and dimensions in order to help raise their vibration. As they see it, their job is to keep energy lines, or meridians, cleansed of pollution and etheric debris. They do so using their fiery breath. Fire cleans out the dross. They do it four times a year, from what he said—at each solstice and equinox."

"And people in ages past worked with them?"

"Yes. Grandfather Adaire had many incarnations as a Druid in Great Britain. He told me that dragons were in the third dimension until the Dark Ages, when they were massacred. They are real, Kendra. And the priests and priestesses who worked with them used telepathy as a form of communication between them. That's why so many myths and legends about dragons exist all over the world. They are still here, doing their job."

"That's what that young man, Miles, told us," Kendra murmured. She sighed and looked at Nolan.

"I'm going to contact Grandfather Adaire about this meeting you had with Eurica," Ana told her. "I don't pretend to know everything about the dragon nation. But it's amazing synchronicity that you met with one just as he was teaching me about them."

"Well, you could have knocked me over with a feather when I realized it was a dragon I'd connected with in that barrow."

"I'm sure. Dragons aren't a part of our everyday reality or culture." Ana laughed.

"I thought I was making it up or dreaming."

"You weren't, Kendra. Eurica gave you specific instructions, and you need to carry them out. I'd like to get back to Adaire and ask if it's possible one or more of these emerald spheres isn't third dimensional. This is a twist in what we know from the legends, and it should be checked out."

"Yes, it should," Kendra agreed. "Listen, thanks for dragonology 101." She heard Ana laugh lightly.

"You're welcome. Here's Calen…."

"Kendra?"

"Yes?"

"It is four days until the full moon. We know that Guerra is around you. The fact that Nolan is picking up on him, or another *Tupay,* verifies that. Reno just suggested that you lead them on a merry chase and confuse them. According to Ana, there are two other *Taqe* strongholds in your area. One is St. Nectan's Glen, the other Merlin's Cave. Both are located near Tintagel, which is supposedly where King Arthur grew up. We want you to drive down there and nose around. We know the *Tupay* can't get into these areas—they can only watch from a distance. Lead them off the scent and make them think the sphere is a good two hours south of Glastonbury. Sound like a plan?"

"Indeed it does." Kendra felt her heart expand. It would mean four days of closeness with Nolan. Little by little, her anger was dissolving, and in its place was yearning—for him. She was reluctant to admit that.

Gulping, Kendra said, "We'll make it happen, and continue to give you daily updates by phone."

"Excellent. Ana says that St. Nectan's Glen is full of fairy folk. They, too, work with the *Taqe*. You might try your psychometric gift there and see if you can connect with them. It can't hurt because we're trying to create a web of alliances among many beings, whether in spirit or the third dimension."

"I understand. I'll do that. Bye."

"Nolan, this place is so magical. You can feel it all around," Kendra whispered as they stood at the waterfall in St. Nectan's Glen. She absorbed his nearness as they paused at the foot of the thundering cataract. The stream was wide, flat rocks in the middle allowed visitors a great view of the well-known fairy glen. Trees hung like a protective latticework over the top of the roaring falls, fifty feet above them. Kendra felt secure and safe in this incredible place.

Everywhere she looked, bright ribbons were hung. Some had contained a child's or an adult's photograph attached, along with a prayer or a request to the fairy folk. Coins had been placed on the moss-covered rocks on one side of the waterfall, as well as cards and treasured pieces of jewelry—gifts to the fairies, in hopes that wishes would be granted.

Nolan grinned, enjoying Kendra's company. They'd walked to a small café at the top, paid their entrance fee and descended a long, winding set of wooden stairs. It fascinated him from a geological perspective that halfway down the fall, all the water poured through a round hole in the stone. A circle. Just like the Vesica Piscis, Nolan thought. The life-giving water gushed through the circle and into the round pond at their feet. Nolan was finding that circles and the *Taqe* seemed to go together.

Kendra glanced up at Nolan, who was studying the beautiful waterfall. They'd driven to Tintagle, had lunch there, and then come to the glen. The day was sunny, a rare occurrence for England, but then, it was early June, one of the most pleasant times of the year. Sunlight lanced through the leaves far above them, reflecting in the stream like golden coins.

When Nolan met her gaze and gave her a slow smile, Kendra felt her heart fill with joy. Maybe it was due to the magical glen, where, it was said, fairy folk came in closest contact with their human counterparts.

Looking away, Kendra murmured, "Has it struck you that, since we both have Irish ancestry, maybe all this stuff about dragons and fairies is right up our alley?"

Nolan raised an eyebrow. "I hadn't thought of it," he admitted, "but it rings true for me."

"Interesting…" Kendra gestured to the wide, wet stones where the gifts and prayers had been placed. "I remember my dad telling me stories about fairies, gnomes, unicorns and the like. I'd forgotten about all that until I connected with Eurica, the black dragon."

"And your dad was from Ireland. Born and raised there."

"That's right." Kendra gave Nolan a soft look. "Now I'm trying to recall all those stories he told me when I was little. I remember some about dragons, too."

"Lots of synchronicity going on here," Nolan asserted. He gazed into her green eyes, and almost felt like he was drowning. Her anger toward him had lessened. He didn't know how or why, but he was grateful. During their time together, he'd felt Kendra growing more and more relaxed around him. Was it possible she might fall in love with him again? He couldn't deny his own feelings.

Nolan's common sense cautioned him to go slowly, and let Kendra call the shots. Let her reconnect with him in her own time and space. But his heart was thundering as she watched him now.

"You know what?" he said. "I remember my grandmother, who was Irish, telling me that whenever you came upon a fairy site, to give them money and make a wish. Fairies like food, grain, coins and pretty objects." He pulled out the pen and notebook he always kept in his left shirt pocket. "I'm going to go over there and make a wish."

"You're such a die-hard romantic, Galloway," Kendra exclaimed with a laugh. "What will you wish for?"

"Oh, no, I'm not telling," he teased, as he made his way across the stones to the damp, grassy bank. "My gram always said if you make a wish, never tell anyone or it won't come true."

Kendra watched Nolan walk to the rock ledge where many gifts had been left. The trees in the glen were all colorfully decorated, reminding her of Christmas. What was Nolan going to wish for?

After scribbling his wish in his notepad, Nolan tore off the page, folded it and placed it on the soft green moss. He pulled coins from his pocket and set them on top. Then he closed his eyes and mentally focused.

"Listen, fairies, I don't know if you really are here, but it feels as if you are. I wish Kendra could trust me again. Please help us repair our past. Help her trust me like she did before the accident. Thank you for whatever help you can swing our way."

Nolan had no idea how else to contact a fairy. His gram had had lots to say about the good fairy folk, but until now, Nolan had forgotten about her stories. As he stood facing the jagged rock, he opened his eyes and looked down at the coins he'd left there. For an instant, he swore he saw them gleam and glitter. And then the shining light dissolved.

Was he seeing things? Nolan realized the slanting sunlight wasn't reaching the rocks where he stood. So what was happening? He wanted to believe the fairies were granting his wish.

Feeling hopeful and humble, he silently thanked the magical beings. Then he turned and gazed at Kendra, who was still standing in the middle of the creek, facing the waterfall. Indeed, there was magic here. He felt it. There was a sense of joy and celebration. This was a happy place, and he was glad to share it with Kendra.

"Nolan? Did you see that light around your coins?"

"Yes. I thought I was imagining things. Now I know I didn't make it up."

She grinned. "I saw a flash of light, and I'm sure whatever you asked for will come true. My dad said fairies represent the light in our lives. He said they are always a blessing, and love to work with us to make our dreams come true."

After taking a deep breath, Nolan sauntered over to where she stood. The spray from the waterfall was cool and refreshing. "That's *great!*"

"So, what did you wish for?"

"I can't say, because I want it to come true." He gazed at her, once again drowning in her glorious green eyes. How badly he wanted to kiss her. To taste her lips once more….

Kendra felt wrapped in Nolan's embrace. Suddenly she ached to kiss him. And she saw the longing in his own narrowed eyes. Something snapped within her, as if buried emotions had cleared. She had no explanation, except that her desire was overriding her wary, distrustful mind.

And then she heard a voice whisper, *"You can trust him...."*

Without thinking, Kendra lifted her hands and framed Nolan's face. She could feel the warmth of his skin beneath her palms. The expression in his eyes made her smile. As surprise turned to heat, Kendra remembered the Nolan of her past—the hunter stalking the woman he hungered for. "I want to kiss you, Nolan," she whispered.

He felt the warmth and strength of Kendra's hands against his cheeks. The golden light dancing in her eyes extinguished any second thoughts he might have had, and Nolan reacted instantly to her tremulous words. Her lips parted, and she rose up on tiptoe, eager to meet his descending mouth.

Nothing had ever felt so right in Nolan's world. Their lips touched, and he felt a bolt of lightning erupt through him. His hands moved of their own accord to Kendra's shoulders, drawing her hard against him. He felt her mouth cajoling his, and a flash of heat followed. All Nolan knew was her hot, slick, sweet mouth moving against his.

In the molten moments that followed, as they became reacquainted with one another, Nolan moved his tongue across her full lower lip. Instantly, he felt Kendra tremble in his grasp. Her breasts pressed against his chest and her red hair brushed his face, tickling him. Her breath was ragged and warm against his flesh.

Kendra moaned when Nolan took her like a warrior claiming his woman. His mouth was strong, cherishing, hungry, wreaking havoc within her heated body. Drowning in his strength, she felt the past dissolve magically. She slid her fingers through his short, dark hair and allowed him to take her full weight, glad when he cradled her securely.

Somewhere in those dizzying moments, Kendra asked herself why she'd held a grudge for so long. Right now, this instant, everything was perfect. They were in tune once more, as they had been so long ago.

She moved her mouth in concert with his. Nolan's breathing was as ragged as hers, their mouths hungrily taking and giving. Kendra felt an avalanche of love for him.

As she stood clinging to this man who had once cherished her, Kendra wondered if they might have a second chance....

Chapter 12

"Why go to St. Nectan's Glen?" Victor asked Hadrian, who sat opposite him at his desk in the Dark Castle.

"Could be part of the trail to the sphere, my lord."

Grimacing, Victor stroked his beard with his fingertips. "When I saw Dr. Johnson from that Aussie's perspective, she looked like she'd come upon something. I could see it in her aura, although she didn't say anything to Professor Galloway."

"What could she possibly have found in that barrow? It was certainly used by Druids in ceremony." Shrugging, Hadrian asked in frustration, "So what else could she have seen or heard in there? Do you think she has the emerald sphere?"

"She didn't. I'd have known. The energy of the emerald sphere is not something I would miss." Clenching his hand, Victor added, "We've *got* to get this sphere! That's all there is to it. The warriors already have two of them. There are only seven in existence. We *must* stop them from acquiring more or our efforts for supremacy will be seriously impeded."

"There are other sacred items out there that can make a difference," Publius countered. "The Emerald Key isn't the only one."

"I agree, but it's like the hub of a wheel, Sir Hadrian. Without it, we're in trouble, though not completely lost. It means we must veer off from our global strategy and swing our focus to finding other powerful talismans hidden around the world. I, for one, want the Emerald Key. It's not referred to as the 'key' for nothing."

"True," Hadrian said.

"I'll inhabit a body every time those two come out of a *Taqe*-protected area. You keep Daria Whitcomb on their trail, but at a distance. There's no way *you* can keep showing up in their lives."

Glumly, Hadrian said, "I know. I thought I had her! Then that damn Galloway got into the mix."

"That's because he's in love with her. I saw indicators of it in their auras." Shaking his head, Victor snarled, "He's like a lovesick puppy over her."

Hadrian smiled. "I can see why. She's a comely woman, Victor, with many fine attributes. She reminds me of a lady I lived with when I was a Greek in the 1400s."

"Don't get snared by a mortal, Sir Hadrian. Especially a *Taqe*. You know better."

"I do," he agreed. "So, our plan is continue to follow them?"

"It's all we can do."

"I wonder what will happen?" Kendra murmured to Nolan as they walked up the well-lit steps to the Chalice Well Gardens. Because they had rented the Michael House, they were allowed to visit after the official visiting hours. It was dusk, the sky a deep lavender on the western horizon. In the east a gleaming full moon was rising.

"I don't know. Just follow your dragon friend's instructions," Nolan told her as they walked up the path hand in hand. He gave her a warm look and squeezed her fingers. "Everything will be all right," he assured her. They stopped and punched in a code in that would allow the huge wrought-iron gate to swing open.

Kendra released his hand and stepped through the gate. She noticed that Nolan was scanning the stone path toward the parking lot. There was one car still there, though all the visitors should have left the grounds long ago.

As the gate locked behind them, she reached out for Nolan's hand once more. Since their magical and healing kiss at St. Nectan's Glen, it was as if they were getting to know one another all over again, this time as mature adults. "I feel like I'm living in a split reality," she confessed in a low voice. "In my professional life, you don't talk to dragons, you don't see light around coins in a glen and you don't go to the Pleiades when you sit in a crop circle."

Nolan nodded. "My grandfather Otis lived in that world, Kendra, so I grew up knowing there were a lot of things around me that I couldn't see and wasn't aware of. All part of the world I walked through daily."

"You're lucky your grandfather shared the information with you."

"Your Navajo upbringing prepared you for this, too," Nolan pointed out quietly as they walked up a slight incline and then down toward the gift shop. From there, they would wander through the gardens to find the two guardian yew trees.

Kendra allowed herself to revel in their intimacy for a moment. The cinnamon scent of yellow roses and then the heady fragrance of red bergamot filled the air around them. For Kendra, the Chalice Well Garden was like the Garden of Eden come to life. "Well, it did and it didn't. The Navajo have a great fear of spirits active at night. That's why they don't leave their hogans after sunset."

"Okay, but what about aliens? Visitors from other stars? Certainly the Navajo have that in their cosmology."

Smiling, Kendra halted near the gift shop, which was closed now. To her left was a beautiful stream flowing over stones, some of which were arranged in two overlapping circles—a Vesica Piscis. "We do. The star people are said to lift humans up, spiritually speaking. We have the Big Star Chant, used for healing. Uncle Henry, who is a medicine man, sings it. He told me many years ago that he'd met star people in the flesh, and they looked like us. I remember my grandfather saying that the star people visit us even to this day. There's a mesa with a portal through which they come and go. Our medicine people meet and talk with them there."

"I'm not surprised," Nolan said as they meandered up the clipped green lawn toward their destination. "So, when you went through that wormhole in the crop circle, you couldn't have been completely shocked at ending up on a star constellation?"

"Yes and no," Kendra answered. "I was never trained as a medicine person in the Navajo tradition. To hear stories of star visitors among us at the reservation is completely different from what I experienced."

"I think it's a shock to your scientist side," Nolan teased.

"I think you're right." She eyed the two huge yew trees that stood on the slight incline. Over three hundred years old, they served as mighty guardians of the garden. "I have to let go of my analytical brain and move into my intuitive side. But I'm worried, Nolan. I'm afraid."

Nolan turned her around, his hands on her shoulders. "Listen," he whispered, squeezing gently, "you do the best you can. We're only human, sweet woman. Yes, there's a lot riding on this, but I know you'll try. If we don't get it the first time around, we'll try again."

"But the dragon said it had to be done two hours after sunset…" Kendra looked at her watch. "That would be in exactly fifteen minutes."

"And if nothing happens, did your dragon say you'd have another chance?"

"Yes, a month from now. Same time and place," Kendra stated.

"Then if that's the way it has to go down, it will." Nolan's heart swelled with love for Kendra. When she had impulsively reached up and initiated that first kiss, his soul had soared with joy. Her action had broken down the wall between them, at least for the moment. Nolan attributed the breakthrough to the fairy folk of the glen, for surely it had been magic that created such an incredible healing between them.

But would it last? It was up to Kendra, not him, to decide that. All Nolan could do was live in the moment and appreciate it. Love was a two-way street.

He didn't want to rush Kendra just because of

that unexpected moment in the glen. Her trust of him was building a little more each day. At Merlin's Cave, they had sat in the middle of the cavern, a tunnel through solid rock opening at one end to the sea, the other to the bay. No doubt, it was an interdimensional passageway between the worlds. The two of them had had a long, searching talk that forged a deeper level of intimacy and honesty between them. Being in that sacred space had helped them view their past with more maturity and less emotion, and he was grateful.

"Listen," Nolan urged, giving her a gentle shake, "you do the best you can. That's all that can be asked of you, Kendra. Okay?" He searched her worried green eyes.

Compressing her lips, she reached up and touched his cheek. "You're so strong in your faith, in your trust of me and this mystical adventure we're on."

"Why shouldn't I be? You're a strong, caring woman with a great heart," Nolan rasped. He wanted to kiss her, but didn't. Kendra had to initiate such things right now. But he ached for her. He dreamed at night of making sweet, wild love with her once more. But he would wait. The trust had to grow stronger between them.

Kendra smiled at Nolan and stepped out of his grasp. She walked over to the nearest yew trees and ran her palm across its thick, rugged bank. "I'll stay in my heart," she whispered. "That's what the dragon

said—to send my love to these tress. She said that
love is the key. The answer."

Nolan stood quietly with Kendra as she ac-
quainted herself with the two mighty trees, which
were over a hundred feet tall and roughly thirty feet
apart. Their lacy green boughs spread outward like
huge arms raised in supplication. "The dragon is
right. She's telling you the same thing Calen and
Reno did. It's all about the heart."

"When isn't it?" Kendra laughed wryly as she
caressed the nubby tree bark.

"I know. We've had rough patches, you and I, but
our hearts never forgot each other."

Nodding, she allowed Nolan's gruff words to flow
through her. Her heart was starting to heal. As
Kendra moved to the other yew, the female one, she
acknowledged that Nolan was once more a part of
her life. Each day with him was tentative, but she was
willing to stay open now and see where it would
lead them. She was scared. Unsure. Kissing him had
altered her life immeasurably, and she still couldn't
understand why she'd initiated it. Trust. She would
have to trust herself and her heart where Nolan was
concerned. A day at a time.

Kendra touched the second yew and introduced
herself, with Nolan quietly following. He was like a
guardian to her; he always had been. And right now,
Kendra absorbed his nearness, his confidence that
she could retrieve the emerald sphere.

Relying on her psychic side rather than facts and logic had kept Kendra off balance. It was Nolan's ongoing belief in her that allowed her to move forward. She didn't want to disappoint Calen or Reno, who seemed convinced that she could locate the emerald sphere. Despite her use of psychometry in her work, Kendra considered herself a scientist and not a metaphysician. Her mother had often kept her from learning about the mystical side of their Navajo heritage in deference to her husband, who claimed that science held all the answers to life's questions.

As she stroked her hand down the trunk of the female yew tree, Kendra could feel the warm presence of the spirit within. She was grateful that her mother had taught her all beings could communicate with one another. Right now, Kendra sensed the excitement and welcome of the stately tree.

"Hey," Nolan whispered, "can you feel these trees? I think they're singing or something." He gave Kendra a wicked grin. "I bet if they could, they'd dance an Irish jig right now. But they're a little root-bound."

Laughing softly, Kendra felt her worry dissolve beneath Nolan's gentle jibes. "You feel the trees, too?"

"Sure," he said, reverently pressing his own palm to the bark. "I can feel their joy. When you touched that male yew, the energy leaped out from him like a huge, happy explosion."

"I'm glad you felt it, too. It gives me more confidence, and I need all the help I can get right now…."

Nolan understood her insecurity. In less than ten minutes, she had to follow instructions given by a dragon spirit. "Sometimes we have to fly on blind faith, Kendra. This is one of those times for you," he said.

He reached out and slid his hand across Kendra's tense shoulders. He could feel her angst. "I don't know of anyone more heart-centered than you. Your love of people, your reverence for all life, is in every cell of your beautiful body."

He saw how her eyes glimmered with tears at his roughly spoken words. Squeezing her shoulder, he whispered, "I know you can do this. I believe in dragons. I believe in the fairy folk. I know they're real." He flashed her a smile. "I'm actually jealous, green with envy that you got to meet a real dragon."

Kendra felt some of her tension dissolve beneath Nolan's gentle teasing. "I wish you could do this instead of me."

"No, the dragon chose you. You're the one, Kendra."

Looking at her watch, she muttered, "It's nearly time."

Nolan released her and stepped back. The dragon had given very explicit instructions on how to retrieve the emerald sphere. Nolan leaned down and retrieved a small limb that had fallen from the yew tree. It was slender, but sturdy enough for the job ahead. He handed it to Kendra. "Use this to draw the Vescia Piscis symbol around the trees."

Nodding, Kendra thanked him. The dragon had

instructed her to find a stick and use it to sketch the symbol in the two trees. She was to center the mighty guardians in the eye of the Vesica Piscis, the part where the two circles overlapped.

There was plenty of room to do exactly that, and in a few minutes, her task was completed. Kendra remained outside the symbol she'd drawn. Already, she could feel a shift occurring. The dragon had told her that the full moon's energy would connect with the Visica Piscis circles and then with the yews. According to the dragon, this amalgam would act like a cascade of power, key to unlocking the secrets of the sphere.

Taking a deep breath, Kendra handed Nolan the stick and then wiped her damp hands nervously on her trousers. The moon was bright, its rays slanting nearly horizontally across the garden. In the lacy boughs of the yews overhead, the light scattered, becoming soft and luminescent. Kendra felt a throbbing begin, and glanced at Nolan, who gave her a thumbs-up. She managed a nervous smile and moved foward.

To ground herself, Kendra visualized tree roots, wrapping solidly around her ankles, then reaching deep into Mother Earth. Just the act of anchoring quelled most of Kendra's anxiety and worry. She felt the heaviness of her body. The connection with the Earth was stabilizing and calming.

The time had come. Taking a deep breath, Kendra stepped into the eye, facing the yews. The full moon glowed brightly upon her. The energy was palpable, and she felt a swirling power unlike any she'd ever experienced. It reminded Kendra of the wormhole, yet it was different. Standing with her feet slightly apart, her knees bent and relaxed, she allowed her arms to hang loosely at her sides. The dragon had told her to hold up her hands toward the moon, and that's what she did. Then closed her eyes.

And it began.

Chapter 13

A powerful dizziness swept through Kendra, nearly catching her off guard, and she steadied herself. The wind whispered softly through the boughs, and she felt it caress her face, as if to reassure her.

She anchored herself more strongly, planting her feet flat against the ground. The dizziness ebbed and flowed, each time easier to deal with. Kendra was glad she'd experienced such sensations before. Sacred, powerful places often sent out invisible waves of energy. But not quite like this. This was concentrated, physically rocking.

Kendra had again asked Nolan not to speak to her, not to interrupt her, during the ceremony. Right now, all she heard was that slight, inconstant breeze. She was sensing the yew trees more and more strongly. On her left was the female, on her right the male. Their energies were very different, but both were powerful.

Then she saw a stream of light begin to rise from near the roots of the female yew. A golden thread, it spiraled around the rugged trunk, then spread and reached toward her, like fingers. Sparkling and golden, it reminded Kendra of a field of tiny stars.

As soon as it made contact, she felt a tingling sensation. The energy from the female yew slowly encircled her from her toes to her head. As it wrapped around her, Kendra felt lighter and lighter, until she seemed to be suspended in the invisible arms of the tree spirit, floating above the ground. She could no longer feel the ground beneath her feet, but was no longer dizzy.

The black dragon had not told her what would happen, only that she was to draw the Vesica Piscis and stand in the eye. Fascinated with what was unfolding, Kendra took a deep, ragged breath as she watched the male yew begin to send its own energy toward her—a bright silver thread. When it spiraled around her, melding with the gold, she felt something completely different.

Heat alternated with coolness in her body. The jacket she wore felt oppressively hot, and she wished for a moment she could pull it off. But then a cooling breeze would whoosh through her and she felt perfectly comfortable again.

Kendra sensed that the trees were balancing her energy in some way. She understood from her training with her Navajo grandmother that a person's aura could often be out of harmony. Everyday life had stresses and strains that affected a person's energy field. Were the yew trees getting her back into balance so that she could access the emerald sphere? Something told her this was a correct assumption.

Focusing on her breathing, Kendra tried to keep it deep and steady. Being centered and calm was essential to working with her psychometric gift. Before long her pulse was throbbing with the gold and silver energies now encasing her aura.

A sound caught her attention. It was far away, but distinct. At first, Kendra thought there was a group of medicine men and women chanting, and she strained to listen. But when it grew clearer and louder, it sounded more like singing.

The screen in her brow switched on, and Kendra saw something that rocked her world. She must be imagining it!

Between the trunks of the yew trees, and across the expanse of the garden, Kendra witnessed what could only be fairies. All kinds of fairies, flitting toward her.

As she honed in on the approaching group, she saw the emerald sphere floating just above them. It struck Kendra that this sphere had gone to the fairy folk for care and protection.

There were so many stories from Ireland about

leprechauns and fairies. In many legends, she recalled, fairies would steal something from a human being. The moment she remembered this, she heard a low, rasping voice near her left ear.

"Dragon priestess, do not think these good beings have stolen anything."

Jumping inwardly, her heart hammering, Kendra nearly yelped in fright, the voice so real. Instead, she swung her psychic awareness upward. The black dragon was hovering protectively above the entire procession, so large she literally blotted out the night sky above the yews. In awe, Kendra noticed how the soft gray of Eurica's scaly underbelly deepened to black farther up on her pear-shaped body. The ancient guardian's glowing black eyes were open, revealing her yellow slitted pupils. Abruptly, Kendra realized the dragon had a close connection with the beautiful, gossamer fairies slowly coming toward her.

"I didn't know you would be here, Eurica. I'm sorry, but you startled me." Kendra sent the message telepathically to the guardian of West Kennett Barrow.

The dragon blew through her large nostrils, releasing jets of white steam that dissoved like glittering wisps in the moonlight. *"At one time, in your life as a priestess of that barrow, you and I worked together. I know you have forgotten this, for good reason, but dragons never forget. The Little People are coming to you with the emerald sphere. It is they whom you must thank for protecting it from the Dark Forces."*

"I will thank them," Kendra mentally replied. *"And I must thank you, as well."*

"You are welcome, my dear priestess and friend. When the queen of the fairies approaches you with the sphere, hold out your hands to accept it. Then thank her. They will remain and sing the sphere into your dimension and into your possession. Right now, it is in the Other Realms."

"I'll do exactly as you have instructed, Eurica. Thank you. I wish I could remember our work together."

"Someday, when you are not so busy, I will come visit you in your dreams, and share with you all that we did together. We were always a good team...."

Kendra believed it. She saw the dragon's eyes gleam and sparkle as the two of them telepathically spoke together. Focusing on the troop of fairies floating like butterflies on a playful breeze, Kendra could now make out what they looked like. Each was unique in face and form, just like humans on Earth. There were males and females, adults and children. Their dress looked translucent, luminescent in the full moon's radiant light. But Kendra did not see wings. Had the tales about them been inaccurate?

"No, my friend. Often, your kind saw them first

*as a dragonfly, butterfly or some other winged insect
or bird. This is how human kind began to equate
wings with the Fairy People. They do not need wings
to fly. They are quite capable of appearing and dis-
appearing from your dimension at will."* Eurica
chuckled, the sound a rumbling of faraway thunder.

In awe, Kendra studied the approaching fairies.
Their high, falsetto voices were joyous, the expres-
sions on their faces akin to rapture as they escorted
the emerald sphere toward her. It glowed with an
inward light and she marveled at the green rays
shooting out of it in all directions. The sphere was
alive and pulsing in harmony with the chanting
voices of the fairies.

The logical part of Kendra's brain, her scientific
side, tried to deny what she was seeing, but deep
down, she knew it was real. The sensation of light-
ness, of hovering over the earth and waiting for the
emerald sphere, chased away all her doubts. Kendra
had no idea if Nolan could see any of what was going
on, but she hoped he did.

The dragon chuckled again.

*"Your companion sees nothing except you stand-
ing there in the Vesica Piscis. He does not have your
sight, but that does not matter. He feels what is happening."*

*"I'm glad. He's very psychic. I almost feel as if
he should be here and not me. His Irish roots are
strong."* Kendra smiled at the dragon.

"Your companion loves you deeply, my friend. It is his love that makes this exchange possible, whether you know it or not. He is as much a part of this ceremony as you are."

Jolted by Eurica's statement, Kendra felt her heart open wider. Nolan still loved her. Somehow, she'd always known that.

"You cannot touch, hold or wear the emerald sphere without understanding love."

Kendra nodded. *"But what if one or all of these spheres fall into* Tupay *hands? They certainly don't come from the heart."*

Erica chuckled again. *"My friend, even if these spheres went to the* Tupay *they would have to first open their hearts to connect with each one. Some can do that, it is true. But many cannot. That is why the Lord of Darkness wanted his daughter, Ana, to wear the Emerald Key necklace. Her heart was not closed as his was. Now, he must try to find a* Tupay *with those characteristics, but that will be very hard for him. Though it is not impossible."*

"And if he does find a Tupay *with such a heart, they could use this necklace, wear it and change the world?"* Kendra asked.

"Indeed, it is so written in the Akashic Records. It does not say who will end up, finally, with the necklace. Only that the Taqe *and* Tupay *both want it. And the* Taqe *have the easiest job, because they work to stay in their heart and the* Tupay *do not. That*

is why the call has gone out from each emerald sphere, in succession, for your kind to come and find it."

The singing rose like a chorus around Kendra now. The gossamer fairies were almost to the trees. Their heartfelt song moved into her ever-expanding heart and she felt their emotions, their joy and excitement.

One of them—surely the queen of the fairies— wore a sparkling, rainbow-colored gown. Her silvery hair was long and flowing, her tresses studded with gemstones of many colors.

No wonder Nolan believed so adamantly in fairy folk! Just getting to see them galvanized Kendra, and now she understood Nolan's belief in them. They were beautiful, heart-centered little beings. Even more humbling, Kendra understood how much they loved Mother Earth. They lived to serve her, tending her plants, bushes and trees. That was their job, Kendra sensed, to be caretakers and help Gaia thrive.

Kendra promised she would never again make snide remarks to Nolan about his Irish beliefs. She now understood his reverence.

The fairies had stopped between the two massive trees, and were looking at her with profound adoration. As the chanting ended and their high-pitched voices died away, the emerald sphere continued to hover above the assembled group, a glittering green sun. Its verdant rays shot out in all directions, flashing constantly, shimmering and vital. Kendra felt the intensity of love on every level as the light washed through her. Everything within its reach was being blessed and fed the heart-centered energy.

In awe, she watched as the fairy queen rose gracefully above the assemblage toward the sphere. Placing her hands beneath the glowing orb, she gazed at Kendra.

"Open your hands now," Eurica instructed. *"The queen will place the sphere in your palms. Once this is done, thank her and tell her that you accept this gift for all."*

Kendra nodded and watched as the smiling queen brought the glowing sphere to her. The emerald was warm, but not burning. As the fairy placed it into her awaiting palms, Kendra mentally thanked her.

The queen bowed and smiled, said nothing and then floated back to her people, who began to sing once more. Their tune was different, but just as melodic, like the call of many birds welcoming the sunrise.

Kendra stared down at the sphere in her hands. It was one thing to see it from afar, but to hold it… She felt pain. And then experienced a shortness of breath. Was she having a heart attack?

"You will be fine, Kendra. When touched, the sphere will automatically clear any blockages, any darkness, or repair any damage done to your heart. It will do this now, because you will not otherwise

be able to stand its energy, once it manifests fully into your world. Just breathe deeply and this process will be over momentarily."

Kendra was grateful to her dragon friend. For as Eurica's rumbling explanation ended, so did the pain, and the sense of pressure in her chest. *"I know I have heart wounds,"* she told the dragon.

"Every human does. None of you are pure of heart as we are. It is something you work toward, and the spirit within this sphere, whose name is Trust, is aware of this. It is the nature of the emerald sphere, however, when held by someone with heart, to heal them. It is the gift the spirits of the emeralds give to humanity once they are received by someone such as yourself."

Kendra's hands tingled wildly as the energy arced up her arms. The sphere seemed to have a dancing golden light deep within. *"I don't feel worthy of holding this beautiful sphere,"* she exclaimed.

"Your humility becomes you, my friend. The emerald knows of the darkness in your heart toward the man who stands behind you. It will mend the hurt now, and you will have the capacity to forgive him and release the past. This, of course, is your choice. The sphere will never make you do anything you don't want to do. Now prepare yourself, for the sphere is going to move from our dimension into yours. In a few minutes, it will appear fully in your cupped hands. Just relax and don't move…"

Indeed, something was happening. Kendra's attention had been fixed on Nolan, their past, and how much she loved him despite what had happened. That awareness left her breathless as the energy flowed up her arms and through the rest of her body. She released those thoughts and memories. The power of the emerald sphere was so great that Kendra felt it in every cell.

Fixing her gaze on the orb in her hands, she noticed something written on the surface of it—a word in Sanskrit, or a similar language. The word was *trust.*

During the next several moments, Kendra's hands became weighted down more and more. As the dizzying power of the green rays flowed ever more strongly, she tried to maintain her focus. The entire world around her turned a dark green color, as if the full moon's white rays had been hidden by a passing cloud. Caught up within the mystical effect, Kendra prayed to her Navajo ancestors for the courage and strength to remain present. Above all, that she not drop the sphere.

Just when she thought she could no longer stand it, a sense of solidity came over her. It started in her toes, then flowed up her ankles and her legs, and beyond. A ragged sigh escaped her lips. *Grounding.* She was coming back into her body, back home. Relief flowed through Kendra as she felt more and more weighty, more and more present. The object in her hands was heavy, solid, real.

"Farewell, my friend," Eurica called. *"I will see*

you in your dreams. Be aware of danger awaiting you outside the garden. The Tupay *want the sphere. I am not allowed to help you. I must return to guarding the barrow. You must trust the man you used to love in order to meet this next challenge…."*

Kendra barely heard the last of the dragon's warning above the rustling of the yew boughs. A cool, damp breeze touched her perspiring brow, and she felt a throbbing in her hands.

Opening her eyes, Kendra looked down. In her palms lay the emerald sphere. It no longer flashed green and gold, but in the moonlight she could see a fire in its depths.

"You did it!"

Nolan's hushed voice was filled with reverence, and Kendra knew it was time to leave. Her heart was wide open as she stepped out and looked at him, the moonlight making it easy to see his excitement and joy.

"Y-yes. We did it, Nolan." Kendra moved toward him. She wanted to wrap her arms around him and tell him she was sorry for the way she'd treated him. But she had the sphere cradled gently in her hands. "Got the pouch ready?"

Calen and Reno had given them a small leather sack line with soft alpaca wool so that the emerald would be well protected. Nolan quickly dug into the pocket of his coat for it, then held it open.

Kendra's fingers brushed his hands as she deposited the sphere, and she felt a flood of warmth. Their kiss in the magical glen at St. Nectan's had begun the healing process. And now, as they stood there, heads bowed and nearly touching, she wanted to kiss Nolan senseless. Fighting the impulse, she whispered unsteadily, "It was so beautiful, Nolan…so incredible. It healed me…healed my heart."

He gave a giddy laugh and secured the strings of the pouch. "It was incredible. I saw the sphere begin to appear, like a soft green light, and then it grew stronger and brighter by the moment. This is so fantastic." Nolan looked at her as he set the pouch fully in her hands. Without thinking, he brushed his palm across her cheek. "You're just as incredible as that sphere," he told her, his voice unsteady and low as he gazed into her eyes. He smiled. Leaning forward, he planted a quick kiss on her lips and then stepped away.

Moved to tears, Kendra stared at him in the silvery moonlight. Her hands throbbed with the energy of the sphere. Calen had instructed her to put it in her pack, which sat on the ground nearby. As if reading her mind, Nolan picked it up, unzipped it and brought it to her.

"Nolan," she whispered as she placed the sphere inside, "my dragon was here. Did you see her?"

"No, I didn't. But I felt something above the trees. It was big and had a helluva presence. Was that her?"

"Yes, yes it was." Zipping the pack, Kendra quickly slipped it on and strapped it around her waist.

She wanted it safe on the short walk through the gardens, down the stone path and across the road to the Michael House. She glanced about in the milky moonlight, which made everything almost like day. "Did you hear the fairies singing? Did you see them?"

He shook his head. "No, I didn't." Quickly, he scuffed at the lines she had drawn around the trees, then took a rake he'd found near the entrance, and erased all evidence of the Vesica Piscis. He didn't want to leave any sign of their being here.

As he worked, he couldn't stop looking over at Kendra. Her face glowed. Her eyes tore his heart apart. She looked so beautiful as she held that magical emerald sphere.

When he'd finished, he walked over to where she waited. Reno had told him that the sphere would magically heal both of them. Hoping beyond hope that that was true, he pointed toward the path. "This way…"

"Nolan, my dragon said there were *Tupay* out there," Kendra warned.

"It's likely true. My birthmark is getting hot."

"They know we have the sphere."

Nolan cupped her elbow and guided her along the stone path, keeping his voice low. "It doesn't matter. We have to get it to the house. Once we're back, we'll call Calen and Reno and tell them we have it." He squeezed Kendra's elbow reassuringly. "Don't worry, I'm here. I'll protect you."

He didn't say what he so desperately wanted to—
that he'd never let what had happened to her sister
happen to her....

Chapter 14

Victor smiled, spotting his opportunity to steal the sphere. The bubble of protection around the Chalice Well Gardens extended to just outside the parking lot. It prevented him from getting in and seeing what had happened. But that didn't matter. He hovered several hundred feet above the couple as they walked hand in hand toward the sidewalk that would lead them to the Michael House.

He could see the green emanations pulsing from Kendra Johnson's backpack. They'd found the emerald sphere! Soon it would be his. He would inhabit her body shortly.

Victor planned to force Johnson toward the Tor,

where *Taqe* energy was nonexistent. The great hill was neutral territory, making it much easier for *Tupay* to act. His accomplice, Christian Campbell, was already in place at the foot of the Tor, hidden in the woods. Knights were a very small cadre in the *Tupay* army and should be used judiciously. Campbell wanted to get even with Galloway, and was resolved to do just that.

Guerra intended to kill both *Taqe,* but wasn't sure when that would occur because of the emerald sphere's presence. Above all, he must get the sphere before Campbell killed Galloway.

That was the wild card in his plan, which was why Victor had told Campbell to wait until called. Because he had the most power, he would place himself in the line of fire. Victor didn't know the gem's full power, and feared some of his plan might not work. He had to act cautiously.

As the couple reached the sidewalk, he struck.

Kendra opened her mouth to say something, but was abruptly cut short. She felt an awful pressure in the region of her stomach, as if someone was pressing a large fist there. She grabbed for her middle. "Nolan…."

Nolan heard the fear in Kendra's strangled voice. He turned to her and saw that her eyes were huge in the moonlight. What was going on? He could see her shock, then felt a dark, heavy, threatening energy. What the hell? He jerked around, the back of his neck burning in warning. Nothing seemed out of place. No one was around. The road was quiet.

Kendra staggered backward, hands pressed against her stomach. Something hissed into her like a snake slithering through her solar plexus and deep inside. The awful feeling of pressure moved from her stomach, through her chest and into her head, then down through her hips and legs, locking into her feet.

Stunned, Kendra couldn't speak. This other presence was within her, and she realized she'd just been attacked. It was the oddest sensation, as if two people were squeezed together and forced to live within one body. And then *his* voice rang in her head like an echo.

"You're mine. You must obey me. Turn and run toward the Tor. Now!"

Kendra croaked in terror. She tried to call out, but the thing that inhabited her stopped her from speaking. Animal-like noises came from her throat, but she couldn't ask Nolan for help. She felt the powerful push within her, felt herself being squeezed into some tiny corner of her body while the malevolent spirit took over. The male was strong, and Kendra knew he could force her to do what he wanted. Still, she struggled to resist.

"Kendra? What's wrong?" Nolan stepped toward her, his hand extended, a question in his eyes.

"I— Help— Something's wrong…." she gasped,

before the being inside her nearly closed off her throat to stop her from speaking. She fought the alien force, but a man's hollow laughter bellowed within her skull. Her heart rate soared; her pulse pounded. Choking, Kendra stumbled backward, pushed by this unknown marauder who had entered her. She had no idea what had happened and her mind spun with questions. With shock. How could she get this thing out of her?

Nolan watched in surprise as Kendra spun around and began to run down the sidewalk. What the hell was going on? At once he set off after her.

When she disappeared around the corner of the brick building, he realized she was taking the route up to the Tor, the dark hill bathed in moonlight above them.

"Kendra!" he shouted, "Stop! Come back!" As he raced behind her, Nolan didn't know what he was running into, only that Kendra was in terrible trouble and he had to help.

Rounding the corner after her, he spotted her across the street, rapidly climbing the path to a gate opening onto the Tor. Why was she going there? None of this made sense!

With a growl, Nolan hurled himself toward her at top speed. She was a shadow running up the dirt path bracketed by trees. Eyes narrowing, panting for breath, Nolan leaped across road and up the path.

And then something else became visible. In the

shadowy path, where the trees arched over, Nolan noticed a lurid red color surrounding Kendra. Was it her aura? It must be, but it scared the hell out of him. She was in desperate danger!

As he ran on, he watched Kendra slip through the gate and continue in long strides up the grassy slope. The colors around her shifted and churned, a menacing presence. Nolan couldn't interpret what he saw, but knew he had to catch up to her.

Desperate, Kendra struggled for control. Fear ate at her as she was marginalized within her own body. The monster within her, whoever he was, had taken over. Yet despite his power, she tried to fight back.

"Stop!" Victor angrily ordered Kendra. She was strong. A lot stronger than any other human he'd ever possessed. Her struggling took a toll on his powers to control her. She was trying to resist him, to slow down. Pushing his energy to maximum, Victor literally threw her past the gate. Stumbling, she fell, and he snarled, *"Damn you, woman! Get up!"*

"Stop doing this to me! I don't want to go anywhere! Let me go!" she screamed mentally.

Guerra laughed. *"Do you know who I am? I'm the master sorcerer, Victor Carancho Guerra. You cannot fight me, woman. You are weak in comparison. Now run. I will control you. You cannot win."*

An icy wave of terror plowed through Kendra as she stumbled upward. The path was narrow and led up to the top, where St. Michael's Tower gleamed in the moonlight. Even her brain felt squeezed, and she could barely think. With her own energy waning, Kendra panicked. Guerra had possessed her. She knew what that meant: as soon as he exited her body, she would die. Emotions avalanched through her as she battled against the sorcerer. She would die and never be able to tell Nolan she'd forgiven him. She would never have time to explore the possibility of loving him once more.

Kendra almost doubled over in wrenching despair. The pressure inside was terrible, as if she were an overinflated balloon about ready to explode into a million pieces. Her skin stretched, her bones expanded to their limits.

She could feel Guerra within her, almost read his intentions. He wanted to find someone on the Tor. And he expended more energy on unbridled rage toward her. She had to resist! Her love for Nolan washed through her like a warm flood, and lessened Victor's iciness.

"Stop that, you bitch! You will never get me out of you until I want to leave!"

Surprised by the fear in Guerra's voice, Kendra tried to think. *Think!* Why was he scared? She slipped again on the damp, wet grass, landing with a grunt on her stomach. At once the sorcerer forced her back to her feet. Her mind was shorting out. Her ability to think rationally was being eaten away in huge chunks by this evil spirit.

"Kendra!" Nolan shouted. "Stop! Wait!" He surged after her, twisting through the gate. A wind arose around the dark, looming Tor. Clouds hid the moon and everything went black. Still, Nolan could see, far ahead of him, the reddish glow that was Kendra.

Kendra felt her body moving against her own wishes, her legs pumping, the breath tearing out of her open mouth. It was the weirdest sensation, to have someone else inhabiting her, controlling her physical body and trying to control her thoughts.

Her spine tingled suddenly, the chill rippling up and down her back turned to warmth. Was that the sphere? She belatedly realized that Guerra had attacked her because she was carrying the brilliant emerald. Of course!

On her captor's unspoken command, Kendra jogged around the base of the Tor toward the woods. She knew the sorcerer wanted her to enter the sinister-looking grove because Christian Campbell was waiting there. He would take the sphere.

It was amazing to know what the sorcerer was going to do. Kendra read every thought he was having, felt every emotion.

The grass was long and covered with dew. She kept slipping on the uneven pastureland. Once again she slowed her steps. Guerra pushed back with a violence that infuriated her.

Her mind swam with desperate thoughts. She had

to stop the sorcerer from taking the emerald sphere. She couldn't deal with the fear of her inevitable death. Longingly, she focused on Nolan.

The instant her mind and heart centered on him, and filled with love, she heard Guerra scream in frustration.

"Damn you! Stop that!"

The warmth in her back became a wave pulsing outward from her heart. It was coming from the sphere in the backpack, Kendra belatedly realized. Suddenly, she understood Guerra's rage. The moment she'd focused on her love for Nolan, he'd lost partial control over her, and she was able to reduce her stride to a walk.

That was it! Kendra remembered what Calen and Reno had said: that love was the only weapon that worked when battling the *Tupay*. She recalled how Ana, the daughter of the sorcerer, had forced him to stop attacking Mace Ridfort, by sending him love.

As the awareness trickled into some dim part of her, Kendra understood what she had to do. The sorcerer was pounding at her energetically, his assaults making her gasp. Falling to her knees, she splayed out her hands, gripped the long, wet grass and desperately clung to it. She had to stop him from forcing her into those woods! Reading her captor's thoughts, she knew Nolan would be shot by Campbell as soon as the Scot wrested the sphere from her pack. Guerra would then exit her body, and she would die, too.

It was a tidy plan, she realized with despair. The *Tupay* would have the third sphere and two *Taqe* would be dead.

Kendra could feel herself dying already, inside her body. She could sense the sorcerer destroying her energy, her personality. Instead of focusing on that, she closed her eyes, her chest heaving from her exertions. With every ounce of strength left to her, she swung her attention to her heart. And her love for Nolan. This time, Kendra held on to that feeling, recalling the rich, joyful time she had spent with him before the loss of her sister.

Guerra screamed. Thrashing violently in the woman's body, he tried to subdue her weakened spirit. The love she was suddenly emitting came toward him in golden waves of light. Guerra feared this more than anything. Sending out a dense, dark cloud of his own, he battled back.

Frustration and rage tunneled through Victor as he divided his energy between forcing Johnson to her feet and blocking the gold cloud of love surging toward him. She fell back onto the ground in a heap. *Dammit!* Guerra saw Galloway approaching, but he didn't fear the man. The archaeologist had no power to stop him even with his telekinetic powers.

But if Victor was overwhelmed by the light, he would have to leave her body. And if he did so, Campbell wouldn't know what had happened. The Scot was out of sight, waiting in the woods, in the darkness. Victor couldn't even communicate telepathically with him, because all his energy was focused on his own survival against this damn *Taqe* woman.

Nolan slid to a halt. Kendra had collapsed upon the ground, and was gripping the long wet grass with white-knuckled fingers. She was groaning, panting raggedly. The lurid red energy swirled around her as he approached, almost as if she were fighting herself.

"Kendra…" Nolan fell to his knees beside her. She was trying to lift her head to look at him. He wasn't sure what to do, so reached out to put his arms around her.

The instant Nolan touched Kendra, a bolt of lightning shot through him, and he was thrown six feet away. After rolling in the wet grass, stunned, he scrambled dizzily to his feet. He stared at Kendra and knew instantly that the sorcerer, Guerra, had possessed her.

The realization shook Nolan as nothing ever would. And then came the shocking truth—that when Guerra exited Kendra's body, she would instantly die. In that moment, Nolan felt totally helpless. It was like watching Debby die all over again—only a hundred times worse. He loved Kendra. They had just found each other once more—and once more, he hadn't protected her.

"No," Nolan whispered raggedly as he started toward her. "No…" He reached out again.

Victor cursed richly. He had only so much power

to discharge as Galloway once more came toward Kendra. Victor didn't want him to hold her or touch her. To do so increased the power of the love she had for this man. When Galloway reached out to grip her shoulder a second time, Victor sent as much energy as he could into the warrior.

The archaeologist was again thrown back, but not as far.

This time, as he'd come forward to try and touch her, Kendra had lifted her head and looked Nolan squarely in the eyes. The terror, the love he saw in her gaze scored his heart. Now, he realized the sorcerer was trying to get him to stop touching the woman he loved.

Deep within himself, Nolan screamed for help. He didn't know what to do, or how to stop her death from occurring. Again he screamed out silently to the cosmos for intervention and help. He had to save the woman he loved.

Kendra honed in on her love for Nolan. Twice, he'd been shocked and driven away by Guerra's power. Even though she would die, she was going to force Guerra out of her. She wasn't going to let him kill the man she loved, nor would she surrender to the sorcerer and let him have the emerald sphere. As she knelt there, feeling the inner tug as her captor tried to force her to stand, Kendra suddenly felt heat explode across her back. Guerra screamed out in surprise, the cry vibrating through her.

Nolan slowly got to his feet, witnessing a green-and-gold light flashing all around them. It was the energy of the sphere! He hesitated, stopping a few feet from where Kendra knelt on the grass. The knapsack was blazing with a blinding emerald light. And then Nolan felt the spirit of the sphere connecting with him telepathically. Without thinking, he lifted his finger and aimed it at the pack.

Guerra shrieked in surprise as the emerald sphere reappeared. Looking to his right, he noticed Galloway standing, his face set, his finger pointed at the sphere, which was now hanging in midair. Thunderstruck, Guerra realized too late that he'd underestimated the man's telekinetic powers. He was drawing the sphere toward his outstretched hand. *No! No!*

Guerra felt torn. The wave of gold light was inching closer. He had to use so much energy to hold it back so that he couldn't stop the sphere from traveling toward Galloway. Frustrated and angry, Guerra didn't know what to do. If Kendra's love overwhelmed him, he would have to leave before it touched him and changed his spirit forever, from *Tupay* to *Taqe.* He just couldn't allow that change to occur. Yet, he needed her. Or did he? He watched as the sphere moved toward Galloway, a glowing globe emitting a radiant green light. He wanted that emerald!

The instant the sphere fitted into his palm, Nolan experienced a surge of energy unlike any he'd ever felt. He gripped the golf-ball-size orb in his fist as the spirit within it telepathically told him to quickly go embrace Kendra. To press the sphere against her heart no matter what happened.

Kendra sensed the sorcerer's decision. As she fought him on every level, she read his mind: he was going to exit her body and attack Nolan. And she would die when he did so.

A moaning cry erupted from her lips and the air hissed out of her lungs. The pressure within her was leaving! Relief flooded her. But in the next instant, blackness drowned her vision and she felt herself falling, falling. She knew she was dying, never to see Nolan again. Never to tell him that she loved him…

Guerra was nearly out of Kendra's body when Galloway held up the emerald sphere. A beam of green light shot out of it and struck the sorcerer, freezing him in place. He screamed in rage. Wresting himself free of the woman, who then crumpled to the ground, he hung suspended in the air, distraught and angry.

What the hell was going on? The sphere had no alliance to anyone! Or did it? As he thrashed about, trying to resist the invisible, imprisoning force field, Guerra realized that there had been a connection between the sphere and Kendra Johnson. She was the first to touch it, to brand it with her essence. It had formed an allegiance to her!

He had a lot to ponder over at this unexpected development, but now was not the time. A murderous expression had come over Galloway's shadowed face. Clearly, he wanted to kill Victor. The sphere was a powerful beacon in his right hand, its green beam keeping the sorcerer trapped. And all the time, Galloway was walking toward Kendra, who lay motionless on the ground.

With one last, desperate struggle, Guerra managed to break free of the green sphere's energy. He sailed up into the moonlit sky, racing away from the two humans. Clearly, he wasn't going to get the sphere now. It had somehow connected with a *Taqe*. Though seriously weakened, he telepathically contacted Campbell, ordering the knight to run out and shoot Galloway. Now!

Guerra stopped and hovered, watching the Scot thunder out of the woods and run across the lower slope of the Tor. In his hand was a pistol. His face was grim, his eyes focused on his quarry, less than two hundred yards away.

Nolan sobbed as he fell to his knees. He set the emerald sphere near Kendra and started to reach for her, then heard a shrill warning inside his head. In the same instant, the birthmark on the back of his neck flared to life. Tearing his focus from Kendra, he spun around.

Campbell was racing toward him, out of the night, gun in hand.

"Not this time, you son of a bitch," Nolan snarled. He leaped to his feet as Campbell halted and raised the pistol. Pointing it at him.

A powerful rage churned through Nolan once

again. He pointed his finger directly at the Scot, who was breathing heavily. The pistol wavered as he tried to aim it, but before the Scot could get off a shot, Nolan released a charge of energy. There was a blinding flash of light, followed by a scream. Campbell was lying on the ground, unmoving, arms splayed outward.

Breathing raggedly, Nolan ran toward him and then quickly scooped up the pistol. As he leaned over the human man he didn't know if Campbell was dead or unconscious, so he shakily placed two fingers against the carotid artery in his neck. No pulse. Campbell was dead.

Straightening, Nolan quickly turned and ran back to where Kendra lay in the damp grass. She couldn't be dead! He had to get help!

Guerra remained at a distance, invisible and watchful. He saw Hadrian's ancient spirit exit the physical body he'd taken over, which was no longer of use to him before it died. His immortality was safe. Cursing, Guerra realized he must go help Hadrian find another body to enter, so that he could continue on the Earth plane. Later, they would have to rethink their plans.

Since three of the emerald spheres were now *Taqe* connected, the other four must be found at once, and touched by a *Tupay*, in order to create an allegiance to their kind. This was an unexpected twist.

Guerra was glad that at least one *Taqe* was dead

in this latest skirmish. One less he and his army would have to fight!

In an instant, the sorcerer was gone.

Chapter 15

Nolan fell to his knees beside Kendra, who was stretched out lifeless on the grass. In the moonlight, her face was ghostlike, her red hair limp. Her eyes were partly open and staring sightlessly. Lips slack, she lay with one leg twisted beneath the other, arms spread outward, fingers curled and bits of grass caught between them.

He had realized too late what had happened—that the sorcerer had possessed her, and then left her body. In his panic, Nolan forgot that he should press the emerald against her heart. Instead, stunned and unable to think clearly, he pulled Kendra into his arms. She was like a rag doll, her head lolling back against his arm.

"Kendra, wake up. Wake up!" He cradled her against his heaving chest and placed a finger against her slender neck. More terror raced through him when he didn't feel a pulse.

With a cry, Nolan shut his eyes and crushed Kendra against him. He had to save her. And he had no idea how to do that except to begin CPR procedures. Placing her on the damp ground, he knelt over her, flattening his hand on her chest, over her heart, and pressing hard. Then he leaned forward, pinched her nostrils shut and fitted his mouth over hers. He breathed his life, his love, into her.

The serrating horror at what was happening almost blinded Nolan as he worked feverishly to revive her. Guerra's possession of her explained why she'd been fighting and grabbing at the grass. Nolan could see signs of struggle in her face, in the flatness of her mouth and the stubborn look in her unblinking eyes. Now he understood. But was it too late?

Nolan labored tirelessly, racking his mind as to how he might save Kendra. But Calen's words haunted him. She'd said nothing could save someone whom a *Tupay* had possessed, then left. That person was dead. Gone.

Hot tears splattered down his drawn cheeks as he worked over Kendra. He wouldn't give up! He wouldn't let her go! Trust had just started to build between them once again. Bitterness assailed Nolan and he breathed deep into Kendra's lungs. He'd said he would protect her this time. The same thing he'd said before their tragic trip down the Colorado River. He'd told Kendra he would keep her and her sister from harm. Well, he hadn't then, and he hadn't now.

Pushing down on her chest, Nolan sobbed aloud. He'd failed her. He'd failed Kendra again.

Gulping, he fought to steady his wild, chaotic emotions. He had to remain calm, so he could keep breathing into Kendra. The moon went behind the clouds again, leaving him in darkness but with tears flooding his eyes, he couldn't see much anyway. Nolan focused solely on Kendra and the love he had for her.

As he continued his ministrations, doggedly and devotedly, he vaguely realized the green sphere, resting beside Kendra on the grass, was beginning to glow. Soon, the emerald light encompassed both of them, in what appeared to be a luminescent bubble. Nolan felt renewed energy, renewed stability, but he never left Kendra, never stopped performing CPR on her.

His heart was bursting with anguish. Time seemed to stand still, as if everything in his life was hanging in balance on the edge of a sword. Nolan couldn't accept—wouldn't accept—life without Kendra. As he leaned over to breathe into her mouth yet again, he became aware of a bright, shining light near her right shoulder. After giving her his breath, he looked up.

"My son, lift her into your arms. If you want to save Kendra, we must go now…."

Gulping back his tears, Nolan saw a kindly looking old man with silvery hair that glowed like a halo around his head. He wore a long beard with two braids on either side with loose hair in the middle. His simple white robe gleamed and sparkled like a cloak of stars. "Who..." Nolan croaked, sliding his arms beneath Kendra's neck and shoulders and pulling her up against him. "Who are you?"

"I'm Grandfather Adaire. We are going between the worlds, my son. It is the only place to take Kendra to try and call back her spirit. Pick up the emerald sphere and place it against her heart. Quickly, for there is no time left."

Nolan dimly recalled hearing about the Village of the Clouds and how it was run by two elders, Grandfather Adaire and Grandmother Alaria. He instinctively knew he could trust this man. The compassionate look on Adaire's narrow, lined face reassured Nolan and he did as the man requested. Reaching out, he picked up the glowing sphere and gently placed it against Kendra's heart.

Adaire's hand was long and thin, but the instant he gripped his shoulder, Nolan felt strength and warmth.

An electric charge shot through him and automatically, he tightened his arms around Kendra. A flash of light was followed by a booming noise. Nolan shut his eyes and pressed his head against hers. Then it felt as if they were moving, so fast that Nolan couldn't even imagine what was happening.

"Open your eyes, my son."

Nolan did so and found himself inside a large, thatched hut. An elderly woman stood nearby, her features worried and tense. She wore a peach-colored shift, her silver hair in thick braids. Nolan assumed she was Adaire's wife.

Carefully, he laid Kendra on the pallet in front of him.

"You need to leave," Adaire instructed, kneeling down beside her. "Go outside and wait. Alaria and I will work to save Kendra. Leave the sphere on her heart. Quickly, now."

Nolan staggered to his feet. He was dizzy and had to reach for the wall. As he steadied himself, Alaria came forward and pressed her finger to his brow. Her healing touch strengthened his balance, and his dizziness disappeared. She gave him a gentle smile and moved to Kendra's side.

Nolan hesitated. He desperately wanted to stay with Kendra. Leaving her now felt like abandonment.

"You are not abandoning her," Alaria told him softly. She pointed toward the open door that led to a kitchen. "Go outside. Try to relax. Let us work to save Kendra."

Moving jerkily, Nolan left the room, his eyes again filled with tears. Barely aware of his surroundings, he staggered out of the hut. Wiping his eyes, he stopped and looked back. If only he could hold Kendra, just to be with her…

"Nolan?"

Lifting his head, he turned. "Calen!"

The woman reached out and touched his shoulder. "Grandmother Alaria came and got me. We're at the Village of the Clouds, the *Taqe* stronghold between the worlds. Come with me."

"But…" He glanced toward the hut where Kendra lay.

"Nolan, if there is a chance to save Kendra, Alaria and Adaire will do so. They are very wise, and thousands of years old. They are great and powerful mystics. They know how to heal better than anyone. If Kendra has a chance of coming back from spirit, it will be with them."

Nolan felt Calen's hand on his upper arm, her fingers firm yet comforting. Blinking back his tears, he rasped, "I didn't realize what had happened. It didn't make sense. I didn't know Guerra had possessed her until it was too late." He covered his face with his hand.

Calen whispered his name and pulled him into her arms. "Oh, Nolan, I'm so sorry. We knew this would be a dangerous mission. We were hoping Guerra wouldn't attack, but knew he could."

Just feeling her strong, warm arms nearly broke him. He buried his head against her body and closed his eyes. Calen patted his shoulder and gently smoothed the material of his jacket.

"W-will they save Kendra?" he asked as he lifted his head and stepped out of her embrace.

"I don't know. There's so much we're learning about the Village of the Clouds."

Nolan glanced around. The place seemed to be full of people of all ages, genders and nations. Children ran around playing with the dogs, which barked excitedly at their heels. Men and women tended cooking pots hanging from iron tripods over fires. The spacious layout of the village belied its importance as a *Taqe* stronghold. This looked like a peaceful community, not a fortress against the *Tupay* high in the mighty Andes.

Calen led Nolan to a hand-carved bench near the hut. "Come on, let's sit down. All we can do right now is wait and pray for Kendra."

The awful knot in Nolan's stomach tightened painfully as he sat down. He could hear birds singing, and monkeys screaming in the distance. He wanted to yell out in terror. Instead, he wiped his perspiring face, numbed by all that was happening.

"What can they do? I just need to understand it all."

Calen sighed and patted Nolan's hand. "There's so much I don't know myself, Nolan. I'm sure the elders will tell you later."

Propping his elbows on his thighs, Nolan buried his face in his hands. What was going on in there? Could the wise ones bring her back? All he could do was focus his powerful love for Kendra, and pray to the Great Spirit to give him one last chance with her, to let her know he loved her more than life. "If I

could, I'd give my life for hers," he said brokenly,
fresh tears burning in his tightly shut eyes.

"I know you would," Calen whispered unsteadily.
"Pray for Kendra, Nolan. Let your love flow into her.
Love is really the only weapon we have against the
Tupay. Send your love to Kendra...."

"Welcome back, Kendra."

The whirling sensation ceased. When Kendra
opened her eyes, she was standing before Calandra
once more. The woman smiled and held out her
hand. Feeling lost in time and space, Kendra slid her
hand into the woman's firm grip. The leader of the
Council wore a pale yellow robe that reminded
Kendra of a Roman toga. On her feet were simple
leather sandals. The elder's handshake imparted a
healing energy. At once, Kendra felt more steady,
more present.

"How did I get here?" she asked. Kendra recognized the gleaming white temple she'd visited before
as she'd sat in the crop circle. Somehow, she was
back here in the Pleiades constellation. Kendra's
mind was fuzzy as she assessed the peaceful temple
grounds. She could hear people's laughter and other
everyday sounds. The pale green sky was now filled
with fluffy pink clouds.

Calandra led her to a white marble bench and
invited her to sit next to her. "Kendra, the Great
Mother Goddess has sent you to us." Calandra

gestured to the sky. "She is boundless and feeds us. We are all her children."

Confused, Kendra wondered if she could be in two places at once. "The Great Mother is well-known to us on Earth, as well. All the ancient civilizations worshipped her before the patriarchy and a new male god replaced her."

Calandra smiled slightly. "That's true. Here in the Pleiades, we went through such upheaval, too. But that was nearly half a million years ago. Now we recognize that the Great Mother cares for all of us, and her consort, the male god, is her partner. Females can give birth and hold life, but we need the other half, the male energy, to complete and make us whole. So long as we are in human form, duality exists, female and male. Those on the Earth plane are learning that only integration of these two energies gives oneness."

Kendra studied the woman. Her silver hair was loose and long, her gray eyes sparkled with life and gleamed with compassion. Kendra didn't even try to guess the elder's age. "What am I doing here?"

"As I said, you were sent to us. We understand that the Great Mother works in mysterious ways. Before your arrival, I was lying down in my home, taking a nap, and I had a dream." Calandra took Kendra's hand in hers. "I saw you standing before me with one of the spheres from the Emerald Key necklace. I heard the Great Mother's voice whispering to me that you would arrive shortly." Calandra smiled. "And so I came here, to her temple, and waited."

"You said you weren't expecting me. What does that mean?"

"Our contact with your planet has been infrequent, and carefully considered," Calandra told her. "Our policy of noninterference is always in place. So often, we watch with deep compassion as your kind struggles with war, strife, epidemics, rape, murder, powermongers—all *Tupay* interests and activities. We can do nothing."

"But why?" Kendra frowned. "What's the point of having so much power and wisdom if you can't use it to help us?"

"Because we must respect the Great Mother's grand design, Kendra. Perhaps one of your Earth's great religions, Buddhism, best reflects her laws. You reincarnate, lifetime after lifetime, to learn not to lie, cheat, steal, rape, murder or use power against another. It is personal experience that teaches you these things. That is what the Great Mother has designed for all her children, no matter where we are in her universal womb." Calandra lifted her toward the sky. "As we learn, our soul remembers each of these painful but necessary lessons. With each new life, we bring information we've gleaned with us. We evolve slowly, over thousands of lifetimes. And become better and better human beings."

"Are all souls created at the same time?" Kendra asked.

"No. The Great Mother is birthing new souls all the time. That is why on your Earth you have very evolved humans and very unevolved ones. The former know that peace is the correct path to follow. Younger souls don't know the difference. They always take instead of give. They like power and abuse it. They are selfish and insensitive, focusing on themselves and not on others."

"And so," Kendra said thoughtfully, "Earth is like an education center where souls go to learn through experience?"

"Exactly!" Calandra smiled widely. "You're a wonderful old soul, Kendra, or you would not be here. And I'm pleased to see you understand the larger vision of our Great Mother."

"Which is why you have the noninterference directive," Kendra said. "Each soul is 'in school' and learning at our own pace. If you interfered, we wouldn't learn what we're supposed to, and we'd stop evolving."

"Yes, you do understand. That's good."

Shaking her head, Kendra said, "And so our war with the *Tupay* will go on until someone wins. If the *Tupay* win, our world will regress."

Calandra nodded. "That is true. But if the *Taqe* win, then the Earth as a whole has a chance to evolve. It will bring all of you closer to peaceful acceptance of one another. Which is a huge step humanity must make in its spiritual development." Calandra patted Kendra's hand. "Do you remember what happened to you before you arrived here?"

Kendra shook her head.

"Master sorcerer Victor Carancho Guerra, the Lord of Darkness of the *Tupay,* possessed your body, Kendra. We watched it happen and we were saddened." Calandra gave her a sorrowful look. "We had to stand by and do nothing. We wanted to stop him, but we could not."

Rubbing her brow, Kendra began to recall that event. It happened in a flash as she replayed the sequence in her mind. "Oh, no," she muttered. Something terrible had happened to her…. She opened her eyes and looked down at her body. "I'm not all here, am I?"

"Your astral body is here with us," Calandra stated.

Kendra's heart contracted with pain. With grief. *Nolan.* She loved him, and she hadn't told him. She drew a sudden breath, almost a gasp, her hand going to her heart. "Am I dead, Calandra? Is that why I'm here?"

"I'm to give you something," the elder told her, not answering the question. "You held the emerald sphere. It is what has brought you here to us, with the agreement of the Great Mother and her master plan. A plan no one else is privy to because we are all still evolving. The Great Mother holds many secrets, and all we can do is surrender to her love and move with faith as she guides us."

Calandra wore a silver necklace with an emerald Vesica Piscis. She removed the necklace and placed it around Kendra's neck. "I was given this in a ceremony thousands of years ago, Kendra. It was a gift from the Great Mother to me. In the dream I had before you arrived, I was told to pass it on to you." Calandra gazed at her. "Now, you become an ambassador, with a direct connection to us in the Council."

The emerald pendant hung between her breasts, feeling warm and solid. She touched it carefully with her fingertips. "This is beautiful, Calandra. So I'm in touch with you now?"

"The Great Mother has decided there will be direct communication between Earth beings and ourselves. We've never had that before. It is a hopeful sign. And you will be the communicator. Anytime you want to speak to me, simply go into meditation and grasp the necklace in your left hand. Will yourself here, to this temple, and I will come and meet you."

"This feels so important," Kendra murmured, holding Calandra's warm gaze. "More than I can begin to realize."

Calandra chuckled. "Yes, but in time, you will grow close to the spirit of this emerald, and it will guide and teach you. Best of all, Kendra, the person who wears this can't ever be killed."

"You mean I'm going to live? I'll see Nolan? I can tell him I love him?" Kendra asked.

"Oh, yes, my dear, that and so much more." Calandra rose and gestured for Kendra to stand. "First lesson—hold the emerald in your left hand and will yourself back to the Village of the Clouds, where your body is presently. It's time for you to go home, Kendra. May the peace and love of the Great Mother be with you…."

Chapter 16

"You may go in now, son," Grandfather Adaire told Nolan.

"How is she?" he asked, rising swiftly from the bench outside the hut. Calen stood, also.

Adaire smiled wearily. "She will live. Her recovery, however, is going to be rocky. Go now." He waved his hand toward the open door of the large, airy cottage.

Nolan didn't need to be told twice. He broke into a relieved grin and thanked Calen for waiting with him, then nearly ran through the door.

Once inside, he went directly to the bedroom. Grandmother Alaria was kneeling over Kendra and pulling a light blue alpaca blanket across her. She gave Nolan a smile as he entered, and gestured for him to come forward.

Nolan only had eyes for Kendra, who appeared to be sleeping. Her face, once so terribly pale, was flushed with color. Her red hair, a flaming halo about her face, was like a testament to life, not death. Quietly, Nolan knelt beside her. They had removed her clothes and replaced them with a simple pink cotton shift, the boat neck showing off the clean lines of her collarbones.

"Stay with her," Alaria whispered as she gently squeezed Kendra's gowned shoulder. "She will awaken shortly. Over on that small table is a pitcher of water and a glass. Let her drink all she wants. She'll be very thirsty, Nolan. And she's going to be very disoriented. Tell her where she is and, most importantly, that you're here and that she's safe." Alaria frowned. "Kendra has been through a lot, energetically speaking. I don't expect you to understand it all, nor will she. When she is improved and walking, you'll lead her to the Pool of Life, which is nearby. That will completely seal her aura, and help her to revive more quickly than anything else could. It is the next step in her healing process."

"Okay," Nolan whispered, reaching out to touch Kendra's other shoulder. Anxiety rippled through him. "She's really going to be okay, Grandmother?"

Alaria nodded and slowly rose. "The Great

Mother Goddess ordained that her spirit return to her body. I have seen this happen only three times in all my years here." She shook her head. "Whether Kendra lived or died was out of our hands, Nolan. We had nothing to do with that decision. Thank the Great Mother, who decided that Kendra should live. She will have a full and complete recovery in less than a month. Her etheric body was badly shredded by Guerra, the master sorcerer. When someone is torn apart like that, we do not have the power to put them back together. But the Great Mother of us all deigned to restore Kendra's spirit."

"Will this change Kendra?" Nolan asked as he touched her bare arm. Her flesh was warm and firm, and he wanted to cry with relief.

Pushing her thin, trembling fingers through her silver hair, Alaria said, "In some ways, it will, my son. Her psychic ability will probably increase. In other respects, well, we'll just have to wait and see. But don't worry, she'll be the Kendra you knew before. None of her memories have been erased or destroyed by this experience." Alaria excused herself and left the room.

Birds were singing melodically outside the open window. The day was warm and comfortable. Nolan could smell the scent of nutmeg wafting in and knew it must be from an orchid hanging in a nearby tree. Turning his attention to Kendra, he settled himself at her side. Gently picking up her hand, he studied her features as she slept.

Oh, how he loved her! Just being able to slide his fingers across hers and feel the warmth of her flesh once more overwhelmed Nolan. As he gazed at her face, her thick coppery lashes lying against her high cheekbones, her golden flesh, a ragged sigh slipped from his lips. They had come so close to death. His stomach knotted and his heart beat harder as he recalled what he'd experienced with Kendra out on the Tor.

Even now, Nolan wondered if she would still love him. Had what she'd gone through change how she felt about him? Everything was so tentative, and all he could do was wait.

And then Kendra's lashes fluttered.

Nolan's breath hitched, his gaze fixed on her face. He watched, mesmerized, as she began to awaken.

Her fingers curled automatically around his. Heartened, Nolan squeezed them gently. Her mouth parted, and she licked her lower lip. Her fine brows twitched and her lashes fluttered again, finally opening to reveal drowsy-looking green eyes.

"Kendra? It's Nolan. You're safe and you're with me," he whispered, getting to his knees and continuing to hold her hand. Leaning closer, he reached out with his other hand and stroked her cheek. "You're okay, sweet woman of mine. Just relax. You're safe…."

Kendra honed in on Nolan's gruff, trembling voice. It was an anchor for her in her floating, semiconscious state. Her body began to feel heavy, and then she became aware of Nolan's warm, strong hand holding hers. A tingle raced up her arm and encircled her heart. When he tentatively brushed her cheek and the line of her jaw, Kendra hungrily absorbed his welcoming touch.

As she opened her eyes, the first thing she saw was Nolan's face and those turquoise-blue eyes of his staring into hers. Why was he so anxious? Kendra could feel Nolan's every emotion, and she struggled to speak. "Nolan? Why are you so worried? I'm fine."

His mouth curved. "Darlin', you look like an angel returned to Earth. I'm so glad." He cupped her jaw and told her where she was. He didn't mention what had happened, not wanting to stress her in any way. All he wanted to do was forge a connection to her, to her heart, if she would allow it.

Kendra sighed and looked around the room at the stuccoed walls and straw thatching overhead. Through the open doorway was another room, but she couldn't see much. It didn't matter where she was, just that Nolan was with her. Inhaling deeply, she whispered, "It smells so good, like someone is cooking cinnamon rolls."

Laughing softly, Nolan said, "It's the orchids in the trees outside, Kendra. I think that's what you're smelling."

Drowning in his burning gaze, she felt more stable and steady with each passing minute. "I'm glad you're holding my hand, Nolan. I'm coming back from…so far away…." Her voice trailed off in confusion. She remembered talking to Calandra, and automatically groped at her chest. There, between her breasts, was the necklace, the emerald Vescia Piscis pendant, that Calandra had given her. It wasn't a dream, after all. Kendra haltingly told Nolan about her second meeting with the woman.

Nolan sat back on his heels after hearing about her journey. "Wow," he murmured, "that's really something. I don't know about you, but I feel like we've stepped into the Twilight Zone and our lives are forever changed."

"I know," Kendra whispered, her voice hoarse. She adjusted the necklace between her breasts. "Help me sit up, Nolan?"

Sliding his arm beneath her shoulders, Nolan lifted her carefully. Kendra leaned against him, her head nestled against the crook of his neck. Just getting to hold her like this sent a wave of exquisite happiness through him. Pressing a kiss to her hair, he whispered, "Grandmother Alaria said you might be thirsty. Do you want some water?"

Kendra nodded, relishing the intimate contact with Nolan. When his arms went around her, she sagged against him and closed her eyes. "Yes, I feel like a camel who's been out in the desert far too long."

Nolan chuckled and pressed a second kiss to her furrowed brow. Just to have Kendra alive and in his arms choked him up. This time, he didn't fight it when tears trickled silently down his face. "Think you can sit up by yourself? The pitcher is over on the table in the corner. I have to get up."

Kendra straightened slowly. "I like being in your arms, but I am thirsty."

Nolan went over and filled the glass. He knelt down and wrapped his arm around Kendra's shoulders once more as he held the water to her lips. She wrapped her fingers around the glass and drank in gulps.

"You *are* a camel," he teased, as he poured her more water. The simple act of helping her drink was a salve to his tortured heart and soul. Kendra was not angry with him. Even though he had not been able to protect her in her greatest moment of danger. Again.

How could Kendra forgive him this second time? Hell, he knew she hadn't forgiven him for her sister's death. Still, Nolan wanted to be here for her, regardless of the outcome. He fully expected her to send him packing once she got well. Until then, he'd be like a starving wolf, absorbing every glance she sent him, each tentative smile. Every moment with her was precious and he wasn't about to squander this time with her.

"This feels incredible, Nolan!" Kendra called as she swam through the warm, turquoise waters of the

legendary Pool of Life. Wearing a bright red bathing
suit, she watched him as he sat on the bank in his
black swim trunks. "Come on in! Grandmother
Alaria said you could do this with me. Come on."
Kendra impatiently held out her hand

How sexy he looked. She felt her entire body re-
sponding to the sight of his tight, muscular frame.
Dark hair emphasized the breadth of his chest, and
she delighted in his broad and capable shoulders.

Nolan gave her a wry, boyish look. Feeling his
hesitation, she waded over to where he sat with his
legs dangling in the healing waters.

"Nolan!" She reached out, grabbed his hand and
hauled him in with her.

With a shout of surprise, Nolan splashed about
awkwardly. Instantly, it felt as if he were in a bottle
of champagne. Thousands of tiny, energizing bubbles encapsulated his body and worked their magic.

Kendra laughed gaily and dived away from him.
The pool was nearly half as big as an Olympic-size
swimming pool, oval in shape and surrounded with
brilliant, blooming jungle flowers. The sun was
warm, the humid air full of musical birdsong.

In seven days, Kendra had bounced back to health
with a speed that took Nolan by surprise. She had
asked him never to leave her side, so he'd slept next
to her. There was no sexual contact. Not that Nolan
didn't want it; he did. But Kendra's healing was far
more important than his own sexual appetite. He was

very clear about his priorities. Nearly losing her had forced him to mature in ways he hadn't before. At the same time, seeing her in a bathing suit that outlined every luscious female curve couldn't help but arouse him.

Kendra resurfaced at the far end of the pool, her red hair clinging to her scalp. A combination of playfulness and desire came over her as she watched Nolan in the waist-deep water, rivulets running down his face. His silly grin made her laugh deeply. She'd never get tired of looking at him.

Seeing the devilish expression in his eyes, Kendra called, "Come on! Take a dip! Isn't this water incredible?"

Nolan wasted no time in diving beneath the warm, clear water. He opened his eyes and admired Kendra's long, shapely legs. All his anxiety, all his dark thoughts of rejection suddenly disappeared. This wasn't like the tragedy on the Colorado River. The water here was healing. It brought them together. Nolan effortlessly swam toward Kendra.

As he pushed off from the white sandy bottom and surged upward, he felt reborn. They had another chance to be together. Bobbing a few feet away from her, he absorbed her winsome smile. This was the Kendra he'd known before all the disasters had reshaped their lives.

Nolan laughed aloud. "This pool is—"

"Magical," Kendra said, finishing his sentence

for him. "It's like all the wounds I had, all the awful memories, the hurt emotions, dissolved when I stepped into this water."

"I feel the same way," he said, looking around at the rippling surface. "It is amazing."

"I wish we had something like this on Earth," she said, moving toward him. "Think of how many people could heal themselves." She slid her arms around his shoulders and allowed her body to float against his. Seeing the look in his eyes, the desire for her, she framed his face with her hands. "Nolan, I love you. I always have. I fought it for so long…so long."

Surprised by her confession, he felt a wave of heat tear through him. When her firm body nudged his, he automatically curved his arms around her waist and drew her close. "Kendra, do you know what you're doing?" he asked with a gulp when she leaned forward to kiss him, a sensuous smile on her face.

"I know exactly what I'm doing, Nolan. Kiss me. Love me, right now." She pressed her mouth against his. At first, she felt him tense, and then his lips took hers, with such hunger that Kendra moaned with pleasure. She felt the sensuality of the man just below the surface, like magma flowing beneath the mantle of the earth. His lips rocked hers open and she felt his tongue move slickly across her lower lip. He tasted of coffee sweetened with honey.

For too long, Kendra had let her anger guide her,

and now the Pool of Life had given her the clarity and the maturity to release those hardened feelings. What was left was the realization that she had always loved Nolan and always would. After dying and coming back to life, Kendra knew what was really important: loving and being loved.

Nolan claimed Kendra's mouth and took her fully into his arms. She floated effortlessly, pressing her womanly hips against him. As her hands worked to push down his swim trunks, he smiled against her mouth.

"Turnabout is fair play, darlin'." He slipped his hands beneath the straps of her suit and drew them downward across the smooth, pliant skin of her shoulders. The beauty of her tall, lithe body, her small breasts and softly rounded belly, was a gift to Nolan.

When they'd removed both bathing suits, they held each other close. Nolan couldn't hide his desire for her and she responded with a smoldering look. It only made Nolan want her more, and he gripped her hands.

An elfish smile blossomed across her lips, and the glint of gold in the green depths of her eyes challenged him. This was the teasing, provocative Kendra he'd known so long ago. His throat tightened and tears blinded him momentarily. He had never loved anyone but her. And now, through some miracle, she was coming to him eagerly, with that familiar hungry look.

"You're mine," Kendra whispered, as she grasped

his shoulders, lifted herself and clasped her long legs around his waist. When her womanly core was pressed against his hard body, she leaned toward him. He held her against him and she felt his lips close over the nipple of her breast. The moment he began to suckle, Kendra moaned and thrust herself down upon his awaiting hardness.

The whole of Nolan's world contracted into one thing: the sensual movement of her hips thrusting against his. This was the wild woman he'd known long ago, and swept him away. Soon he was lost in a haze of pleasure, tasting her lips, running his fingers through her wet, tangled hair, breathing in the essence of her unique fragrance.

Kendra moaned as he teethed her nipples, his hand moving around to cup her most sensitive area. Her entire body convulsed and she threw her head back, her neck exposed to the sunlight. A shattering, rippling explosion began deep within her and spread out like glittering rings of fire. If Nolan hadn't held her, kept her captive against his strong, powerful body, she would have fainted from the ecstasy of their coming together.

And just as Kendra saw the lights dancing through her body, the starbursts and explosions, she heard him growl her name. He dug his hands into her hips and they clung to one another, the reverberations of their joyful coupling moving through them simultaneously, like an earthquake. Kendra reached out and gripped Nolan's bunched shoulders, felt his power and litheness as he hauled her against him, his mouth finding hers.

Their lips clashed together once more. Oh! It had been too long. Kendra saw a limpid haze of rainbow colors as she floated, eyes closed, with Nolan captured within the hot confines of her body. Heart bursting, she felt as if she was being reborn. It was a celebration of all that was wonderful about a man and woman coming together in love.

The water surged around them as Nolan's knees buckled. Kendra weighed far less in the water than she would in the air, but a delicious weakness was flowing through them. Unlocking her legs from around his hips, she murmured, "Let's go lie down together on the shore."

They uncoupled and he led her out of the water and up the grassy bank, where they collapsed together, laughing. Nolan pulled her back into his arms. Her wet, slender body folded beautifully against his and he cradled her close, their breathing still ragged.

"Helluva welcome back," Nolan said with a deep sigh. Strands of her hair tickled his nose and chin, and he grinned. Stroking his fingers across her damp, sleek shoulder, he kissed her hair, her temple and cheek. Her eyes were closed and she was smiling. That tender expression touched Nolan's pounding heart. He'd given her that look of satisfaction. All that was male within him soared with joy at being able to give Kendra his love.

The sunlight caressed them and the breeze played with Kendra's drying hair. Nolan watched, mesmerized, as the strands turned to burgundy, then gold and crimson, depending on which way they were teased and blown. She was like that to him—scintillating, ever changing. Nolan pressed his brow against hers. "I love you, Kendra Johnson. Now. Tomorrow. Forever…"

Kendra sighed and slid her palm across his cheek. "And you are the only man I've ever loved or will love. Why was I so bullheaded, Nolan? Why did I waste nine years of our lives we could have spent together? Looking back, it seems like such a stupid choice to make."

Easing away, Nolan studied her face and saw the regret. "Listen to me, darlin', we all make choices. We think we're right when we make them. I did break your trust, Kendra. You had a right to be angry at me. I would have been, too." Nolan's voice grew strained. "I forgave you a long time ago, Kendra." And then he smiled. "The fact you can forgive me now makes me feel like living again. I broke your trust twice. I couldn't protect you against Guerra, either. I'm so sorry about that."

Seeing the hurt, the frustration in Nolan's shadowed eyes, Kendra reached up and kissed him. "You did the best you could. No one could protect me against that sorcerer. I know you wanted to."

Nolan sighed. "Yes, but I felt so damn helpless. And scared. Our issues have always been about trust. Trust of one another when things go wrong. I failed you twice. I don't ever want to fail you again."

"Nolan, don't do that to yourself." Kendra placed her finger against his beautiful mouth. She wanted to love him all over again. "No one can always keep another person safe. It's impossible. The important thing is you tried. *Both* times. And I see that now."

Knowing how she felt, that she'd forgiven him, filled him with relief. Another burden that he'd long carried disappeared. "Maybe we just had to grow up, Kendra. I know I've done a lot of maturing since we split up. Looking back on that horrible day, I realized I should have asked local raft companies about the condition of the river. I'd gone down it so many times that season, that I'd assumed and it was a mistake. A terrible one. There was no way for me to know the adverse conditions we'd face in the river." Nolan shook his head, frustrated by the past.

"I know you had rafted down that river many, many times. What no one could know was a thunderstorm happened and the water runoff loosened a boulder that fell into it. Even if you had talked to locals, it could have happened after they'd floated that station of the Colorado, Nolan. At the time, I refused to factor all those possibilites in. I was grieving at losing my whole family so quickly, in such a short span of years. I didn't deal with it very well and blamed you for it." Kendra stroked his cheek. "I'm so sorry I did that to you."

"Well," he whispered, tunneling his fingers through her hair and bringing her cheek against his, "it's behind us now. We've grown, we've gotten wiser with age." Easing her chin up, Nolan settled his mouth against hers.

But before he got too lost in Kendra, he had to get the words out. "Marry me, darlin'? Let's spend the rest of this life together."

Chapter 17

"This is a historic moment," Calen Hernandez told the five people seated at the round, mahogany table. The initial construction of the new building was complete. Bright sunlight slanted through the window of the room where they sat. This would be their planning space, a place to work on strategy for retrieving the rest of the emerald spheres.

She looked around the table. To her left was her husband, Reno, fondly gazing back at her. On her right was Mace Ridfort, dressed in jeans and boots, a hydrology engineer who dug wells throughout South America to help poor villages get clean water. His work was critical for reducing infant deaths that plagued that continent. Next to Mace sat his wife, Ana, who had just returned from the Village of the Clouds and another marathon session studying metaphysics with Grandfather Adaire and Grandmother Alaria. Ana gave Calen a quick smile of hello. Dressed in a soft pink blouse, white linen trousers and sandals, her black hair was drawn back into a ponytail.

As Calen gazed around the table, she met Professor Nolan Galloway's stare. He had just arrived from Britain less than four hours ago with the green sphere, and his jet lag was evident. Next to him was his partner, Dr. Kendra Johnson, who seemed equally exhausted. Her red hair was in mild disarray around her face and shoulders, though she wore a businesslike beige pantsuit.

"The moment is historic," Calen repeated in a low tone, "because it fulfills an old Inca legend. It said that six *Taqe* would come together in the name of peace. Three couples, all Warriors for the Light. And that when they convened, the energy would be set at this point and locked in with the *Tupay,* the Dark Forces who want to plunge this planet into a thousand years of chaos." She looked around the group once more. "This is the first official meeting of the three couples mentioned in the legend."

Reno leaned forward, his elbows on the table. He gave Calen a tender look, then swung his attention to the others present. "We've already been tested. We've all tasted battle with the *Tupay,* and with their leader, Guerra. We all know from experience that the *Tupay* play for keeps. They will kill to get their hands on any portion of the Emerald Key necklace." He saw everyone's head dip in agreement.

Nolan said, "We're at an interesting intersection, having all of us here, no question. And a very provocative one, I think." Turning, he gave Mace a long, searching look. "Are you aware that your last name, Ridfort, has Templar origins? Gerard de Ridfort was grand master of the Knights Templar from 1185 to 1189. The Templars were part of the Order of our Lady of Scion, sometimes just referred to as the Order of Scion."

Mace shook his head. "No, I wasn't. Just because I have the name doesn't mean I'm from that lineage."

"True," Nolan admitted, "but was your father French?"

"He was," Mace said, frowning.

"Well, Ridfort is French. You might do some research and check your genealogy."

Ana gave her husband a proud look. "See? I was right—you *are* a knight in shining armor. You come from a family of knights!"

The others chuckled indulgently and the tension was broken. Mace flushed briefly and looked over at Nolan. "What are you implying here?"

With a shrug, Nolan said, "The Templars were outlawed by the Catholic Church because they believed Mary Magdalene was the wife of Jesus, and possibly even had children resulting from that union. This was all underground, supersecret information, of course, but once the church got ahold of it, they made sure the Templars were past history. What makes this a provocative investigation is to wonder if the Templars were in fact Warriors for the Light. Did they carry the birthmark of the Pleiadians? Because if they did, then the Templars may have been our forebears, in a manner of speaking. You might be the modern-day equivalent, Mace."

Reno eyed Mace with new interest. "I think it's valuable having two archaeologists in our midst. It's interesting that you may have descended from a Templar, Mace. What that may mean, we don't know yet, but it's another thread in the tapestry we seem to be weaving together."

Ana smiled softly and looked around the room. She placed her hand on her abdomen. "Well, it might be important, because I found out just this morning that I'm pregnant."

Calen clapped her hands and whooped with joy. "Congratulations, you two. The second part of the prophecy has just come true! It was said the woman to wear the Emerald Key would be with child."

Reno grinned, reached across the table and shook Mace's hand. "Great news."

Ana grimaced. "That means we have nine months to find the other emerald spheres. That isn't long. And can we do it in that time frame?"

Some of the joy of the moment evaporated as they all sat there looking at one another. Calen finally spoke.

"We already have three of the spheres. And we found them in three months' time. We have four more to go." She looked to Reno. "Go ahead and fill everyone in on our plan."

Reno clasped his large hands together. "I've been in touch with another member of the Jaguar Clan of shape-shifters—Major Mike Houston. He's very famous down here in South America. At one time, he was a U.S. Army Special Forces captain, and later waged war in Peru against the drug lords. He fought them for seven years with Peruvian Army soldiers he trained. After that, he joined Morgan Trayhern's supersecret organization, Perseus, in Montana. Houston became coordinator for all missions originating out of this underground CIA affiliate."

"And he is a jaguar shape-shifter?" Ana inquired.

"That's right. His mother was a Quero Indian from Peru, and his father a North American military officer." Reno smiled briefly. "Over time, Houston created a sub branch of Perseus known as Medusa— Houston's baby, dealing with paranormal events. He's been able to utilize his own knowledge in the area to help out on some specialized missions. Morgan Trayhern, who founded Perseus, doesn't have that background or understanding, lets Mike run it."

"That's not unusual," Nolan said. "A lot of people don't believe in paranormal events."

"Right," Reno agreed. "When I talked to Mike last week, I filled him in on who and what we are. He was happy, to say the least, to hear of another organization that was pro-paranormal. I asked if he could come down here and help us set up a mission command system like the ones at Perseus and Medusa. And he agreed to do that. Houston is due here tomorrow." Reno glanced around the table. "All of you are invited to sit in with Mike as he teaches us the ropes. He's aware of the prophecy about the Emerald Key necklace. And he understands the importance of what we're doing, so he's throwing his considerable weight and support into helping us."

"Excellent," Kendra said. "Nothing like having someone from the trenches teach us in a hurry what we need to know."

"We got lucky," Calen agreed. "And speaking of luck… Reno set up our Web site several months ago, and we've found a number of applicants who have the Vesica Piscis birthmark. I've hired ten employees to deal with these inquiries, run background checks and so forth. We will then determine who will go after the fourth emerald sphere."

"Things are really coming together," Kendra exclaimed. "You and Reno have been busy while we were out in the field."

Nolan cleared his throat. "This seems like an appropriate time to share a little good news from Kendra and me, if I may?" He grasped Kendra's left hand. "We're engaged to be married. This red-haired woman has agreed to tie the knot with me."

Clapping and cheers erupted around the room. Nolan looked proudly at Kendra, who was smiling widely. Her green eyes glowed with love. As he held up her left hand for all to see, he told the group, "After we left the Village of the Clouds, we decided to stop in Cuzco. I know a good jeweler there, and Kendra fell in love with this pink diamond."

Calen leaned forward to look at the sparkling diamond set in gold. "Breathtaking."

Ana examined it next, then sighed. "That is just gorgeous, Kendra. Congratulations to both of you."

Kendra withdrew her hand and glanced warmly at her fiancé. "Thanks, everyone. Nolan and I decided to bury the past and live in the present. So there's hope for archaeologists who live in the past by trade." She chuckled with him over the insider's joke about their career.

"Wise choice," Reno said. "I think all of us have wounds from the past that haunt us until we manage to clean out our emotional closets."

"Haven't we all had that problem?" Calen said with a wry twist of her mouth. "And toward that end, we have a schematic for our growing organization we'd like to share with you." She went and retrieved a pile of purple folders, then passed them out. "Reno and I created this concept with help from Mike Houston. We're using Mike as an overseer of sorts on our setup phase. He's already approved this portion, but we need you to look at it and see if you agree with how we're going to use each team's skills and talents."

Calen looked at Reno. "Your turn."

"Go ahead and open the folders," he said. "You'll see Top Secret stamped on each page. Only folks with this level of security clearance will be able to access these files. We've hired four people, checked them out securitywise, and they will be working with us shortly, with top secret clearance, as well." Reno glanced at Mace, who was project engineer for the new building. "We should be up and operational in about two weeks, right? We still on schedule, Mace?"

He nodded and tapped his watch with his index finger. "On schedule, Reno."

"Having an engineer in the ranks sure is useful," Calen said with a smile. "Okay, Reno, let's look at job assignments. See if everyone likes what they'll be doing."

"Sure," he said, thumbing through his copy. "Okay, Mace and Ana—" he glanced over at them "—we're assigning you the following. Unless you don't like it, or don't think you can handle it. Let us know. Today, we'll hash out the core organizational priorities, because this whole foundation hinges on the six of us."

"Right," Mace said, reading rapidly through the job description.

Reno looked around the table. "Calen and I envisioned three departments for the foundation—missions planning, information retrieval and thirdly, the paranormal. We've tried to assess each of your abilities and support your strengths. In some areas, you may be weak, but working in them and gaining experience will turn a weakness into a strength."

"So, Ana and I are going to be your paranormal department," Mace said. He smiled at her. "Perfect match, don't you think?"

"It is," she declared. "I like the part where we'll be working directly with the Village of the Clouds and creating a similar paranormal school here." Her own smile widened. "I love to teach!" She looked at her husband. "Mace? Are you pleased about this?"

"Very," he said. "And we'll be teaching our little one…." He eyed her belly with satisfaction.

"Oh," Calen said with a chuckle, "Two out of the three couples at this table will be teaching children, plus handling our foundation jobs." She winked at Reno, since she was three months along herself.

"I think having a family is fine, just not now." Kendra shared a look with Nolan.

"I'm in agreement," he said. "Too many digs to go to in far-flung parts of the world. Where there might not be medical facilities if something happened to a child. We'll look at starting a family when we're not such tumbleweeds."

Calen smiled. "I can just see the children you

would have. They'd take after you and probably become world famous archaeologists, too."

"I think kids should have nature as one of their teachers," Kendra stated.

"No disagreement there," Mace interjected. "I grew up in the jungles of Peru. It has made me a better person."

"A wonderful knight."

Mace gave Ana a look that had her blushing. "As long as I can be your knight, my lady, that's all I want out of life."

"Well spoken…!" Nolan looked down at his file and then at Reno and Calen. "We're the information section, eh?"

"Yes," Reno said. "You're our experts on symbology, on archaeology, on ancient languages and history. Going after these last four spheres, we're going to need both of you and your extensive backgrounds. You'll draw together relevant information before a team heads out on a mission, and then be available if they stumble into something they don't know about out in the field."

"I like this," Kendra said, excitement in her tone. "It's a well thought out plan. You have used our strengths."

Calen grinned at her husband. "See? I told you it would work out."

Raising his thick black brows, Reno gave a mock bow in her direction. "As always, you are right."

"Speaking of being ready," Nolan said, "have you had a dream about where the next emerald sphere is hidden, Calen?"

"I did," she said briskly. She pulled a drawing from the back of her folder. "Take a look at this sketch, everyone. Where do you think this is located, Kendra and Nolan?"

"Why," Kendra said, "this is the Great Serpent Mound near Dayton, Ohio. This next sphere is in the United States!"

Nolan nodded. "Nice job, Calen."

"What is that?" Ana asked.

"An earthwork of gigantic proportions that resembles a crawling snake holding an egg in its mouth. It was built during the Hopewell period in the U.S.," Nolan said, "by people known as the mound builders."

"But there's little information known about that period or those people," Kendra told them.

"Well," Reno said, "we've got a possible team ready to go. We need to sit down with them, assess their skill sets, and then vote on whether we think they're the right couple to go after this sphere."

Nolan pursued his lips. "Sounds good to me. They've got the Vesica Piscis birthmark on their necks?"

"Yes," Calen said. "Both of them do. But more on them later. Right now, we need to move to other topics...."

* * *

Kendra was glad the four-hour meeting was over. She walked hand in hand with Nolan down the hall of Calen and Reno's three-story condominium. They each had a bedroom on the second floor, but had opted to stay together. Nolan opened the door for hers and she stepped into the large suite. Sunlight filtered in through gauzy white curtains at the window.

"Nice to be home, isn't it?" she said as she sat on the gold-and-red-striped couch. Leaning down, she removed her shoes.

Nolan shut the door and sauntered over. He sat on the ottoman in front of the couch, facing Kendra. "It is. How are you doing? You've got dark smudges under your eyes. Are you all right?"

Touched by his concern, Kendra reached out and squeezed his hand, which was resting on his thigh. "Never better. I'm just tired from that long flight. I'm still adjusting energetically to everything and I didn't sleep well on the plane. I never do. Flying is such a stress these days."

Nolan absorbed her glorious red hair and golden features. "Let's order up some hot tea and scones. Maybe take a nap together afterward?" He held her warm gaze and felt his lower body tightening with need of her.

Every night was a delicious dessert, as far as he was concerned. It was as if almost ten years of being separated were made up for each time they came together in love. And their lovemaking was intense. Even now, Nolan looked forward to having Kendra in his arms again.

Placing her shoes to one side, she ran her fingers through her slightly curly hair. In the high humidity, it was more wavy than usual. "Sounds good to me." She looked at the pink diamond solitaire on her finger. "You know, Nolan, I can't dig with this beauty on my hand."

"I know, darlin'. You don't want to lose the stone. You can always give it to me to keep in my pocket." He grinned.

"I'll do just that." Kendra sighed and glanced around the sumptuously designed suite. The wallpaper was a pale yellow, to celebrate the sunlight flooding through the large floor-to-ceiling windows. There was a gold-and-burgundy duvet on the king-size bed with gleaming mahogany dressers to match. The lamps on the bedstands were Waterford crystal, with pale lavender shades. Best of all, Kendra liked all the greenery in the room, from the lush palm in the corner to a twelve-foot guava tree in a black planter. Several pots of colorful begonias were placed artfully here and there.

"You know what?"

Nolan cocked his head. "What?"

"I'm really happy, Nolan. I'm happy to be with you. Happy that our past is put to rest." Kendra reached out and grasped his hand again. She gazed

into his dancing blue eyes and saw love mirrored in
their depths. "I'm really looking forward to spending
the rest of my days at your side." She swallowed,
feeling choked up suddenly. Wiping away her tears,
she whispered, "You saved my life with your love."

Nolan shifted to the couch beside her and draped
his arm around her shoulders. He sensed Kendra was
very tired and needed to lean on him. And that's
exactly what she did. "Darlin', I'm so happy I could
burst," he murmured, pressing a kiss to her hair.
Inhaling her scent, he closed his eyes and simply held
this woman he loved so much.

Kendra eased her arm around his waist, content
as never before. "Since my near-death experience,
everything seems so different, Nolan. I feel like I can
almost read your mind. In that meeting today, I was
picking up on everyone's thoughts. At least, the more
important ones." Kendra sighed and nuzzled her head
beneath his chin. "Grandfather Adaire said that
anyone who goes through such an experience has
their psychic senses changed and rearranged. I
believe him. I was seeing colors around everyone.
I've always heard of people saying they could see
auras, but now I am, too."

"That might come in handy, you know? We have
a new team about ready to go after the next sphere.
We're due to meet with them tomorrow afternoon.
You can look at their auras, listen to their thoughts
and see if they're right for the mission."

Laughing, Kendra slid her fingers to the top button of Nolan's shirt. "I think it's going to take me time to understand the psychic gifts I've been given." She eased the button open, exposing a bit more of Nolan's dark, hairy chest. "Right now," she murmured, "all I want is some time alone with you."

"You've got it," he whispered as he tunneled his fingers through her hair. "Come on. What do you say we lie down on that bed and see what happens?"

Kendra laughed softly and pressed her palm to his chest. "I can feel your heart beating…."

"And it's yours, darlin'. Forever…"

* * * * *

*Look for Lindsay McKenna's next romance,
available from HQN in December 2008!*

REQUEST YOUR FREE BOOKS!

2 FREE NOVELS PLUS 2 FREE GIFTS!

Silhouette®

nocturne™

Dramatic and Sensual Tales of Paranormal Romance.

YES! Please send me 2 FREE Silhouette® Nocturne™ novels and my 2 FREE gifts. After receiving them, if I don't wish to receive any more books, I can return the shipping statement marked "cancel." If I don't cancel, I will receive 4 brand-new novels every other month and be billed just $4.47 per book in the U.S. or $4.99 per book in Canada, plus 25¢ shipping and handling per book plus applicable taxes, if any*. That's a savings of about 15% off the cover price! I understand that accepting the 2 free books and gifts places me under no obligation to buy anything. I can always return a shipment and cancel at any time. Even if I never buy another book from Silhouette, the two free books and gifts are mine to keep forever.

238 SDN ELS4 338 SDN ELXG

Name	(PLEASE PRINT)
Address	Apt. #
City	State/Prov.	Zip/Postal Code

Signature (if under 18, a parent or guardian must sign)

Mail to the **Silhouette Reader Service™:**
IN U.S.A.: P.O. Box 1867, Buffalo, NY 14240-1867
IN CANADA: P.O. Box 609, Fort Erie, Ontario L2A 5X3

Not valid to current Silhouette Nocturne subscribers.

Want to try two free books from another line?
Call 1-800-873-8635 or visit www.morefreebooks.com.

* Terms and prices subject to change without notice. NY residents add applicable sales tax. Canadian residents will be charged applicable provincial taxes and GST. This offer is limited to one order per household. All orders subject to approval. Credit or debit balances in a customer's account(s) may be offset by any other outstanding balance owed by or to the customer. Please allow 4 to 6 weeks for delivery.

Your Privacy: Silhouette is committed to protecting your privacy. Our Privacy Policy is available online at www.eHarlequin.com or upon request from the Reader Service. From time to time we make our lists of customers available to reputable firms who may have a product or service of interest to you. If you would prefer we not share your name and address, please check here. ☐

SN07

Silhouette® Desire

Buy 2 Silhouette Desire books and receive

$1.⁰⁰ off

your purchase of the Silhouette Desire novel
Iron Cowboy by *New York Times* bestselling author

DIANA PALMER

on sale March 2008.

Receive $1.⁰⁰ off

the Silhouette Desire novel IRON COWBOY,
on sale March 2008, when you purchase
2 Silhouette Desire books.

*Available wherever books are sold including most bookstores,
supermarkets, drugstores and discount stores.*

Coupon expires August 31, 2008. Redeemable at participating retail
outlets in the U.S. only. Limit one coupon per customer.

11470

5 65373 00076 2   (8100) 0 11470

SDCPNUS0208

Silhouette® Desire

Buy 2 Silhouette Desire books and receive

$1.00 off

your purchase of the Silhouette Desire novel
Iron Cowboy by *New York Times* bestselling author

DIANA PALMER

on sale March 2008.

Receive $1.00 off

the Silhouette Desire novel **IRON COWBOY**,
on sale March 2008, when you purchase
2 Silhouette Desire books.

Available wherever books are sold including most bookstores,
supermarkets, drugstores and discount stores.

Coupon expires August 31, 2008. Redeemable at participating retail
outlets in Canada only. Limit one coupon per customer.

52608214

Silhouette

nocturne™

COMING NEXT MONTH

#35 LAST WOLF STANDING • Rhyannon Byrd
Bloodrunners

Mason Dillinger is caught between two worlds, yet belongs to neither. While hunting down a rogue Lycan, he rescues Torrance Watson. But taking a human life-mate defies the laws of both worlds, and Mason finds himself fighting a battle he can't win, for a passion he can't live without....

#36 BEAST OF DESIRE • Lisa Renee Jones
Knights of White

Only in the throes of lust and battle does Des embrace his dark side. But in protecting the lovely Jessica from the Darkland Beasts, it is the knight that must rule. Yet the darkness is getting harder to contain. Can the one woman who can tame him for all eternity do so before he steals the very life she's destined to share with him?